Lion

SONYA WALGER

 **New York Review Books** New York

This is a New York Review Book

published by The New York Review of Books

207 East 32nd Street, New York, NY 10016

www.nyrb.com

Library of Congress Cataloging-in-Publication Data
Names: Walger, Sonya, author.
Title: Lion / Sonya Walger.
Description: New York: New York Review Books, 2025.
Identifiers: LCCN 2024025990 (print) | LCCN 2024025991 (ebook) | ISBN
    9781681379036 (paperback) | ISBN 9781681379043 (ebook)
Subjects: LCSH: Fathers and daughters—Fiction. | LCGFT:
    Autobiographical fiction. | Novels.
Classification: LCC PS3623.A35875 L56 2025 (print) | LCC PS3623.A35875
    (ebook) | DDC 813/.6—dc23/eng/20240614
LC record available at https://lccn.loc.gov/2024025990
LC ebook record available at https://lccn.loc.gov/2024025991

ISBN 978-1-68137-903-6
Available as an electronic book; ISBN 978-1-68137-904-3

Printed in the United States of America on acid-free paper.

10 9 8 7 6 5 4 3 2 1

For Billie and Jake

Lioness

BUT HOW HARD to be the one who stayed! The one who packed the raisins but not the nuts, who wiped the lipstick off the piano teacher's mug, tissue-wrapped the Christmas ornaments, washed the sheets, staunched the blood, ignored the lies and the slammed doors, peeled the stickers off the walls, fought for sunscreen and table manners, made beds, combed out the lice, stapled the hems and later sewed them, kissed the friends, befriended the lovers, returned the books, loaned the car, the house, the denim jacket with the Liberty lining, combed out the lice, listened to the story tape jammed in the car stereo, held back the hair bent over the loo, paid the school fees, paid the tennis coach, paid the airfare, combed out the lice, pushed the swings, paired the socks, allowed the cigarettes, forbade unkindness, packed the trunk, renewed the passports, taught the second tongue, recited the alphabet, churned the ice cream, bought the bras, the Walkman, the wedding dress, learned the names and never forgot them, shared the crossword, the towel, the chewed gum. The one who did not stray, who was always where I left her, who never spoke a word against him, who signed birthday cards in his name, lied in his name, raised a human in his name.

And here I write a book about the one who left.

She tells me this is a betrayal. She tells me she did her best. I tell her she did, that for better or worse, this book is not about her. No one can be two parents. I tell her my writing is not a measure of her failure, or of anyone's failure. It is a book about love.

My mother tells me she will never read this.

I will write it anyway.

I would not be here without her.

Father Christmas

TOMORROW MY BOY TURNS SIX and five days later my girl turns eight. This means that for five days each year, I have two children who are only a year apart. They are oddly reassuring, these five days, the number somehow a validation of how hard it was in those early years, how inexpressibly exhausting to have two children in diapers, two children in cribs, two children sobbing in the night. What this nearness in age means for them is a deeply competitive week of comparing birthday gifts, parties, cards, love. It makes the whole family anxious. We are all relieved when it's over. This morning we stood at the fridge again, staring at the printouts of the month of February. Each kid has their own calendar to decorate and desecrate. My son needs more explanation about the difference between the *party* and the *actual birthday*. The party will consist of two Covid-tested friends who will clamber into a vast inflatable house my husband has sourced from the Internet, play with Legos outdoors, and eat a *Star Wars* cake while sitting six feet apart. We will shower him with presents to mitigate the lack of friends, family, and festivity.

But today, the children are fractious, anticipatory, exhausted by the slow crawl through the day. The improbably huge bouncy house shimmers in the garden. It is an obstacle course, with a towering slide and pillars to climb. It is bigger than our house, and the children seem lost in its vastness. It is obscenely lonely, dominating the garden, eclipsing the tiny budding cherry tree, and only seems to amplify everything else that is missing from the day. I go to pick up my son's cake. It is gray with white stripes, small as a helmet, utterly bleak. I feel deflated. I remember I am supposed to cover it with plastic Lego figurines, that the frosting is just the backdrop, that I ordered it this way. This feels somehow deeply metaphorical but I am too tired to probe it further. I drive home, numb, listening to a meditation podcast. The host has the voice of a hypnotist. She talks about living an embodied life. She talks about the trance of living at speed and how it stops us from inhabiting our bodies in the here and now. I wonder how old this episode is. Who is living at speed right now? I live in a sun-dazed shuffle.

I am five and six and seven. I spend most weekends with my grandmother. Her house is white with a driveway that crunches and there are enough rooms for the whole family. The sofa is furry deep beetroot pink with thick gold tassels. My grandfather is fierce. He keeps his teeth in a glass, watches cricket with me in his lap, and mutters when I ask to watch the Muppets. My grandmother's house is the house everyone comes to. In the summer it smells of tennis balls and lightly fizzy fruit salad and the soft waft of sweet peas. In the winter it is piney and cold and there is a sprig of holly over every single painting in the long hallway. A tiger skin sprawls on the wall up the staircase and under the stairs is the freezing bathroom with a small paned window the gardener once climbed through to help me when I locked myself in.

When I return for the weekends, everything is where I left it. My books and toys live in a chest under the window in the room that belongs to my aunt but is really mine. There is a jewelry box in her bottom drawer that has a rope of orange beads and a photo of a man with a long white beard. It smells woodsy and ripe and foreign. My mother cries when she catches me playing with my aunt's beads so I hide the beads and wait till after dark to pull them out again. In the kitchen there is a blue tin that always has sweet biscuits in it. I never lose at Snap, Memory, or at anything in this house.

My birthday is in June and always at my grandmother's house. I wear underwear and my red rain boots because in the summer, grass snakes hide in my grandmother's deep lawn. It is hot, sprinklers hiss, the pool hiccups, and my friends and I play Pass the Parcel in the long grass. We have swum and screamed and now we must play games until it is time for cake, but inexplicably here is Father Christmas. He walks around the side of the house as though he lived in it. He is carrying a blue flower in a red pot. He waves at me. I stay quite still. My mother smiles and encourages me to run over. I walk slowly. My boots squelch. I am white-bellied with red boots. He is red-bellied with white sneakers. Behind me the girls squeal but I move slowly. He sits down in a garden chair and places the plant on the ground beside him. He beckons me over. I feel the girls jostling behind me. He is not the right shape but my mother is smiling. I edge a little closer; there is pushing behind me, and squealing.

"Happy birthday," he says. He hands me the plant.

I take it. No one has ever given me a plant before. It is bushy, each blue head like a firework made up of small round flowers. I wonder why he has brought me a flower and not a toy. I feel grown-up and disappointed.

"Thank you," I whisper.

He reaches for me so I climb onto his lap. The robe is scratchy and hot. He is thin like a birch, not sturdy like a Christmas tree. His voice is warm and soft and there is whiskey in it. He smells like my grandfather on Sunday nights. I do not know this skin. This is a voice I do not recognize. I want to go upstairs and climb under my sheets and wait for him to leave. But I cannot. Because it is Father Christmas and he has come in the middle of June for my birthday and that is so special and no one else gets Father Christmas on their birthday and look he brought you a hydrangea and isn't that special and now the other girls hug his knees and he scoops them up and throws them gently one at a time into the pool and the party goes on and he folds in among the grown-ups who pretend to be so surprised to have Father Christmas in their midst but they are not really. Later he brings out my cake. It is not a cake, it is a tart slick with fat red strawberries. The candles wobble in the custard and won't stand up properly. I wonder if my mother thinks it will be more fun to have a tart than a cake like the time she thinks it is more fun to send me to school with green-and-blue-striped tights instead of normal blue ones, or the time she lets me and my friends dye my mother's hair instead of the Girl's World Styling Head and then doesn't wash it and fetches me from school with pink hair. And then when I weep and beg, she wears a silk scarf wrapped around her head instead, which is worse. One of the mothers asks her if she would ask Sonya's mother for a playdate. She thinks my mother is the nanny. My mother loves this story. My mother likes that we do things differently. I do not.

We lick the red glaze off our hot hands and wipe it on our towels. Out of the corner of my eye, I watch Father Christmas walk into my grandmother's house. I never see him come out again. The birthday party dissolves. My friends fold into the backs of cars and shriek goodbyes from the driveway, my mother's friends linger and clink in the sunset. One man laughs loudly and my mother strokes his cheek. The evening grows damp like a towel. I sit under the rhododendron bushes that skirt the lawn, picking at the gelatinous strawberries stuck to paper plates. My grandmother retrieves me from the leafy darkness. She takes me upstairs and bathes me in her tub, soaps my hair and never once gets it in my eyes. And much later, as I lie in my bed, I wonder, why did Father Christmas come and not my father?

Beginning

KINSHASA. I don't even know where it is. I have to look it up on a map.

My father, who is not yet my father, arrives there at the end of summer. He is twenty-six. He has been sent to secure a deal to produce the new banknotes for the newly minted Republic of Zaire, formerly the Democratic Republic of the Congo. It is not clear how he has procured this contract nor from whom, nor what possible qualification he has for it. He stays in the only large hotel in town. It has a pool, air-conditioning, and a casino. It is where the foreigners stay, and meetings are held, and imported liquor is guaranteed. In the lobby the sex workers linger, in the dining room the waiters wait. Everyone is waiting for something. He goes to his room, orders a drink.

"Whiskey," he says, and, lest he get sent a quantity he cannot afford, he specifies, "in a glass."

"*Comment?*"

"In a glass. *Un verre.*"

My father's French accent is swamped by his Argentine one and he must repeat himself several times. Solemnly, an African

arrives at his door bearing a bottle of Johnnie Walker, a bucket
of ice, and a small pat of butter.

My father secures the deal. Money changes hands. He is
invited to stay until the banknotes arrive. My father has
nowhere else to be and the invitation carries an undertone that
he knows to obey. The Congolese have paid but the banknotes
do not come. Back in Buenos Aires his contact no longer
responds to calls. The phone rings and rings. The Congolese
Treasury is waiting. His money is running out. The Congolese
Treasury is losing patience. He is an Argentine abroad for the
first time. He has high cheekbones and long limbs. He is on
the cusp of everything. He swims laps in the empty pool, wonders how in the world this will end. He begins to feel he is
being watched. He spends more time in the lobby, in the bar,
in the casino, places he can see and be seen. He takes up black-
jack. A white girl runs the table. She has dark hair and an accent
he cannot place.

"Newcastle," she tells him. "In the north of England."

She is anomalous enough in this strange world that her for-
eignness makes her familiar. There is nothing to do but sleep
with her. They become lovers, secretly, she could lose her job
for this. He tells her of his predicament, stuck here waiting for
banknotes that are never coming, in over his head and without
an exit strategy. She slips him some chips and he buys himself
another week. When her shift ends, she takes the employee
elevator up to his room. One night some Congolese men play

at her table. She overhears their conversation, keeps her face as neutral as the two of clubs. Later my father joins. She never glances at him but at the end of the hand slides him a pile of chips he has not won.

"Run," she whispers.

He cashes in the chips, retrieves his passport from the front desk and walks out of the hotel with only the clothes he is wearing. He takes a cab straight to the airport. He boards the first flight he can find that is headed somewhere Spanish-speaking.

The next morning he arrives in Madrid.

My mother leaves home when she is five years old. Her parents are English colonials. They live in East Africa and send all four of their children back to England to boarding school. My mother survives this journey by taking care of her youngest sister, who is three. (To this day my mother is a nursery-school teacher, as though destined to endlessly soothe and comfort the abandoned child newly in transit to education.)

She is sixteen. She is done with boarding school, done with being told what to do. Her parents have returned to England and she studies for her exams at home. My grandmother, guilty at having missed so much of her offspring's childhood, and grateful to be involved in her daughter's life, helps her study. Together they decline irregular French verbs, read Tolstoy and García Lorca.

My mother is accepted to the University of Madrid to study Spanish. She is elated. She is eighteen.

A cousin offers her a flat share in Madrid. She moves in with her, begins studying, finds a job translating in the afternoons. She is shy, golden, teetering on womanhood. She comes home for Christmas, yawning with the exhaustion of independence. She is full of Spain and her studies. My grandparents gift her a secondhand car, a canary yellow Mini that she drives slowly back to Spain through a blizzard over the Pyrenees, my grandmother beside her for company. It takes them days. They arrive at the flat she left a month earlier to find it is now occupied.

She has heard he'd be staying. The cousin has written over Christmas that a family friend needs her bed over the holidays, but he'll be gone before she gets back. She has folded the letter up and told no one, wondering who this person might be, lying in her new sheets, looking at her dresses hanging in the cupboard, her long necklaces draped off the mirror. She has wondered idly, then tucked it away. But now, pulling up outside her flat, shivering her suitcase up the stairway, her mother at her back, key in the lock, the lights on, stumbling over a man's shoes in the hallway, a man's shirt on the floor, the sound of the shower running, now she flickers into sensation: Now, now is when my life begins.

My father spends Christmas in Madrid. His family has family here, a distant cousin with a flat, an empty room he can use over the holidays. He lies low, nervous of reaching out to anyone lest word get back to Kinshasa. He dines on tapas and red wine, rising gracefully from outdoor tables and evaporating into the evening without paying. He waits for money from his employer, then his parents, for word from the Congo, for what in the world to do next. He has left home with a flourish, an exotic job, and a fortune teller's prophecy that greatness is coming ringing in his ears. He is not ready to fail. And he has no idea what to do next.

He spends Christmas Eve in a movie theater. He goes back to the borrowed apartment, idly rifles through drawers. Among the cousin's underwear he finds a roll of pesos. He unfurls several notes, pockets them, carefully replaces the rubber band. He opens a bottle of wine, turns on the radio. In his bedroom the dresses sway. They smell of the woman in whose bed he sleeps. He sprays her perfume. It is already familiar. Photos in plastic frames of a family, a tall father in a uniform, a mother elegant, quiet, direct in gaze. A brother with an easy smile, two sisters, one round-faced, cautious, the other blond, tongue blaring at the world. Ropes of necklaces and a dish with gold hoops. A stack of books by the bed and in the bedside table the blue tissue of airmail written in an elegant hand. He pulls the letters out, lies back on the bed, and reads them.

"Darling girl," the letters begin, signed "Mum." None from Dad. A couple from a younger sister, and one from a girl called Susie who describes boys with names so English that he feels foreign again.

His cufflinks now clink beside her earrings in the little dish.
His one tie hangs among her necklaces. Her bathrobe, pale
pink with tiny sprigs of blue, hangs on the back of the door.
He tries it on. It is tight across his shoulders. He puts a hand
in the pocket, pulls out a carefully wrapped piece of chewed
gum and a yellow hair elastic. He makes himself an espresso
and pulls one of her books off the shelf. A Chilean poet, the
most famous, full of love and longing. Underlined with earnest
precision. Ragged on a corner, a scribbled Madrid phone number. He reaches for the phone, dials the number. After several
rings a man's voice answers. He hangs up, throws the book in
the trash. He thinks about calling the other English girl he
knows, the one in Kinshasa. He thinks about what she risked
by telling him to leave. He does not call.

He is in love with her long before she arrives. The strands
of her blond hair wrapped around the black hairbrush. The
clean scent of her shampoo. The fur cap on the back of the
door, the carefulness of her round script, and the big white
house her parents stand in front of. She is from somewhere.
She belongs to a world that is reliable, that is in its right place.
She smells of money. Not a fortune, not ruinous, but comfortable. Everything about her is comfortable. So when he slides
out of the shower and hears women's voices in the other room,
he closes his eyes, runs his hands through his wet hair, smears
the steamed mirror to check himself, arranges his towel, and
thinks: Now, now is when my life begins.

My grandmother stays on for another week. No one remembers where. What is certain is that neither my mother nor my father moves out. My father has nothing to do and nowhere to be. It is as though he has been created by the gods and dropped in my mother's living room. He is beautiful, urbane, solicitous. She is eighteen, inexperienced, a dove. He drives her lemon-drop Mini with careless ease and astonishing speed. He drives her to classes, to her job, to dinner. It is heady. She must have felt like life would always be like this.

The cousin returns sullen, dismayed, jealous. This has not been foreseen. The charming Argentine, her brother's friend, is not supposed to have fallen for her flatmate. She watches them make each other coffee, steal back to bed, stifling laughter. Then silence echoing from the tiny guest room. They try to include her—join us for dinner, for a walk, for a movie. She shrugs, remote and rigid with jealousy. They run free into the icy mouth of Madrid's winter.

Three months later my mother calls my grandmother to tell her they are engaged.

My grandparents ask her to come home. She quits the university, her job, the flat, after less than two terms, and together they drive back to England. They make it in half the time it took her just three months earlier, my father now at the wheel, impatient for his new life to begin.

A cautious welcome from my grandparents. Separate bedrooms. A friendly dinner. My grandfather ushers my father into the living room. Sits in his chair and gestures my father to the fireplace. My father looks around for a chair but cannot see one so he pulls up a footstool. He sits at my grandfather's feet and waits.

"Is this a shotgun wedding?" my grandfather, the colonel, asks.

My father looks unsettled.

"I don't own a gun," he says.

"Is she pregnant?"

My father assures him that she is not. He offers himself to my grandfather for inspection. He is a lawyer, he tells him, with his own apartment waiting for him back in Buenos Aires. He comes from a respected family that will welcome my mother. His own mother is a lawyer and a judge, his father a businessman who spent several years working in India, where my maternal grandfather, the man he is speaking to, happens to have been born.

Twelve weeks of courtship.

Two continents, two languages, and eight years between them.

One month later they are married.

My father can go home now, all questions about his future, or his past, swept aside by the presence of his impeccable English bride. And she can stride into adulthood, bypassing the indignities of adolescence, no need to wait for the telephone to ring, to cringe as her father intercepts a call, to wait for letters and dances and army boys to remember her name. They have both leapfrogged into the unassailable world of grown-ups. And they are deeply, astonishingly in love.

My mother arrives newly married in Buenos Aires to discover that not everything is as it has been described. Her husband is not a lawyer but several exams shy of even completing his degree. The apartment he lives in is not his own, but shared, and owned by a wealthy school friend. My father's parents are doting intellectuals who, enchanted by my beautiful well-bred mother and relieved at their son's good sense, scramble to find and furnish an apartment for them. The make-believe of newly married life begins.

My mother arranges her wedding china. She carefully writes her thank-you letters, hands them to my father to mail. They never arrive. He shrugs, blames the poorly run country, never admitting he thrust them in a trash can in the Plaza de Mayo rather than queue for stamps. My father goes back to school. My mother gets a job, of which my father disapproves. He stays out, spending long nights at his mother's house, where political debates bloom late into the night. A spotlit table, my father's mother presiding, plumes of smoke and tiny brimming ashtrays, half-drunk bottles of wine and espresso cups of silver so thin you can dent them with your thumb, men raising arms and eyebrows and voices, my grandmother implacable, nodding, sucking on her cigarette, all of them fixated on returning an exiled politician to power, an exiled politician and his dead wife who will restore democracy, will feed the masses, while in the kitchen the exhausted maid props her head in her hands as the calls for more coffee echo off the tiled walls.

My mother finds a gun in their apartment. My father tells her that he is looking after it for a friend. He leaves early for the university, returns at dawn. Sometimes he smells of alcohol. Always cigarettes. She calls her mother, tells her nothing. She gets a puppy. His friends stay the night and leave without saying goodbye, a rumpled blanket on the sofa and a dirty glass in the sink. My parents watch the news together, her feet in his lap. One night a photo appears on the screen of a man wanted in connection with a political killing. It is the photo of a man who stayed at their apartment. She looks at my father. He pours himself a glass of wine and changes the channel.

My mother has few friends. My father's friends are terrifying to her. Not the earnest revolutionaries with their middle-class manners, these men are civil, solicitous, but the women, Amazonian, lethally slim, with their seventies bodies and long arched spines. My father's mother throws a cocktail party for the newlyweds, urges my mother to wear her wedding dress since none of the guests attended the wedding. My mother, wide-eyed, accommodating, agrees. My father's social group is small, cruel, perfectly honed by decades of inbreeding. He has dated every eligible young woman in his environs, and they all accept the invitation to view the interloper. They arrive, elegant, bare-armed, honey-skinned, all dipped in their jeans, careless of their boyfriends, offering both cheeks for a kiss in the national gesture of welcome, inhaling cigarettes and exhaling disdain. My mother wears the dress that weeks earlier was so beautiful and now is a too-tight costume. She is an ostrich among sleek wolves. She is a sacrificial virgin encircled by golden vipers. She hides in the bathroom and weeps, pulling at her wedding dress.

She makes a friend at work. They walk the city together. She goes with my father's parents to their country house, a patch of land my grandfather bought and built slab by slab with his own hands. As a boy my father helped him dig the swimming pool. My mother is peaceful here. My father's sister is kind and has young children she can dote on, and here my mother feels at home. She is pregnant. My mother and father are happy. They lie in bed and pick names, plan a nursery, wonder which language their baby will speak. To secure their baby's British citizenship, they decide to give birth in England.

My mother lumbers onto a plane. She leaves her life behind her, violets in a vase on the table, her wedding china in the cupboards, milk in the fridge for her husband who is to join her shortly. She plans to come back with her new baby. She never sees that apartment again.

She returns to her parents' house, finds a doctor who will deliver her, and waits for her husband and her baby to come. It is early summer in England. The lawn is green, her mother brings her tea in the mornings, the lazy light spills through her bedroom curtains, and there are no golden vipers here, no fugitive men sleeping on the sofa. Her husband arrives. He is breathless about England, about his baby, about the opportunities that might await him here. He goes out at night, to meetings, appointments, dinners. My mother's parents ask her where he is. She tells them meetings, appointments, dinners. Already she has doubts. Already she must hide them. She is twenty-one. She has no one to tell. Her friends are still at university, still stumbling drunkenly from one party to another. To whom will she say, What have I done, what have I done, what have I done. To whom will she say, I do not know where he goes at night, this man to whom I pledged myself. It is a secret shame she cannot share, even with herself.

One night the pains begin. She wails in the bathtub. Her mother wipes her brow. My father is out. No one knows where. My grandparents drive their trembling aching daughter to the hospital. She clenches her hands. Where is her husband? The nurses, the doctor, the grandparents, everyone is asking. Dug down inside her, deep as a baby's crown, is the terror that he is with another woman. It makes her sweat with pain. Deeper than a baby's fist is the thought of him with another woman, a woman with vowels from the north, whom she chanced to overhear on a phone, who may be in England now, now as she is splitting open alone in a clinic, holding this secret, ripped open with the terror of her world tearing apart. She bites down. And the baby will not come. The baby will not come into a world that has no father in it nor emerge from a mother who is so alone. The baby will stay locked in place because this is not a family yet. The doctor turns to forceps because this baby will not come and must be dragged into this fatherless world. And then my father runs into the hospital, tearing down corridors, slams into my mother's room, and she is weeping and he clasps her hand and buries his face in her hair and she will never ever know because she will never ever ask and my grandparents turn their faces away and now, now I am ready for my life to begin.

Ending

I AM ONE AND A HALF. We live in a borrowed flat in London. My father goes to Vietnam. The war is over, the Americans are leaving en masse, abandoning all their artillery. There is a fortune to be made, he says, in scrap metal. He will gather it up and sell it back to America, and they will buy it, he says jubilantly. They will buy their own tanks back from him! In a photo he poses, jungle behind him, bucket hat at a rakish angle, one foot on a lopsided tank. In London, my mother waits with her baby. She is twenty-three. There is only one flight a week from Hanoi. Every week she fills the fridge with salami, cheese, cornichons, with the salt that he loves. Every week he does not come. He does not call. He does not telegram. The lion is in the jungle. One week she works late, she cannot do her weekly grocery shopping. She leaves money with her brother, who is visiting. He is another renegade, a blond joker with an easy smile who recognizes his dark twin in his brother-in-law. She asks him to babysit and buy the things on the list, because this is the day her husband is coming home, she knows it. She returns home late to find her brother asleep on the sofa. She opens the fridge. He has stuffed it entirely with toilet paper. Every shelf is wadded with white rolls. He can think of no other way to shock her out of her delusion. He opens one eye from the couch.

"Let him eat that," he says. "You know he's not coming back."

He does come back.

But the marriage is over.

Monster

I am working in the north of Oregon. I have not left the children for more than a week since they were born. Now I am gone for two weeks, almost three. The children are reproachful, outraged. My daughter says she has not slept since I left. I call them at bedtime and we read to each other on the telephone, our faces squished against tiny screens. I tell them I love them; I recite elaborate relaxations for them to help them sleep. I send golden light through each toe, ascend it around their calves, balloon it into their bellies, let it hang like a cloak from their soft spines. I entertain myself by finding new verbs for each body part, and they breathe softly next to their screens. My son can fall asleep with my voice in his ear. My daughter needs to feel the heat of me beside her and only then can she release her hummingbird body. I miss their morning breath and sweaty heads, their devotion at bedtime, their disinterest on waking. I wonder how my father lived without me. I hover between the luxury of surrender to work and the emptiness of my arms.

I wonder who I would be if my father had owned an iPhone.

My father is five. His parents gather in the hallway, surrounded by suitcases. His sisters push past him, cling to their parents' legs. My father's father crouches down, holds the girls tightly. He stands and pats his son on the head. They will be back in a month, they say. The English governess and French Mademoiselle will look after them. They must go to India for work. A month is not so very long says my father's mother, snapping her handbag. They leave. The children wait. Months pass. The children have everything they want and nothing they need. They grow wild. The governess is strict. The children turn over tables, climb trees. Mademoiselle locks them in their rooms. They break free. They forget to wait for their parents. They speak three languages now but invent a private one for each other. My father climbs into his sisters' beds to sleep. He steals from the French lady's purse. She catches him. She drags him out to the barn. It is pitch-dark there and bats shuffle in the rafters. She pushes him to his knees. She tells him to stay there, on his knees, till she returns. She turns the key. Tiny bullets of corn lodge in his fat knees. The darkness is fetid and it rustles. A single thread of white light slices the floor, and at the padlocked doors are my aunts' hot mouths pressing, breathing, waiting, powerless. A whole day he waits on his knees in the dark.

My father who fell from planes and shot through windshields shudders whenever he tells this story.

My father's parents take this trip three times. Each time they leave for a year. Each time they tell the children they will be back in one month. Each time their children believe them.

I am four and five. I live with my mother. We live in the flat above the nursery school where she works. It is cold and nothing quite works because we have no money. My room has a dresser with drawers that don't close and the fridge is empty. We walk across the street to the baker with the pale blue awning and buy a whole apple pie and eat it, still warm, for dinner with spoons at the kitchen table. She teaches me to read. I lie in her lap with books. She cries often. I am all she has. I am her most precious thing. She gets migraines and then her door is closed and you must not even knock you must manage darling. I play downstairs in the nursery school. When the children are gone it is mine and the toys are mine and the puzzles and all the books and also the red skirt threaded with silver that I can wear to bed if I want to because you don't have to share anything if you're on your own. But when the children are there I must share everything, even my mother.

It is the afternoon. A friend has come to play. We are upstairs in our flat above the school. I am dressed as a Native American, in my favorite trousers that have the yellow fringe down the side. I have no shirt on because Native Americans do not wear shirts. In the kitchen hangs the bridesmaid dress that my mother has ironed. I will wear it tomorrow. I am often a bridesmaid because my mother's friends are getting married at last and there are no other children. My friend and I play hide-and-seek. It is my turn. I hide in the kitchen, beneath a shelf. I crouch into myself, waiting. My skin is nut-brown and smells of sunlight. The electric kettle sits above me. I can hear it boiling. My mother always makes jelly for my playdates. The kettle clicks off. I wait. My friend comes into the kitchen, hesitates. Now she sees me. She cries out. I come out from my hiding place and I feel a tug on my foot and it is tangled in the cord and now there is a hot sudden weight on my back and the kettle is on me and hot water is falling and steaming and my back is screaming in hot water. There is screaming. There is a bath full of cold water and me sitting in it and my beautiful trousers staining the water brown and my mother is holding me and still the screaming does not stop. My face is in the sofa with its soft blue-and-white ticking and it is sticking to my face and the screaming and my mother's voice, offering me fizzy drinks, offering me ice cream, offering me anything to make the screaming stop, but the screaming cannot stop, and how, I wonder, am I supposed to eat anything in this moment with all this screaming and then there are sirens and men with clear straight voices.

I am alone in a room in the hospital face down in a bed. My back is burned to the base of my spine. I am alone because the risk of infection is so high. One nurse and my mother are allowed to see me. They feed me bitter pink medicine, which

I refuse to take. They ask what will make me take it. I tell them to bring me a milkshake because that is the most outrageous thing I can think of. I drink a milkshake every day. I ask what the bad smell is and they tell me it is the medicine. No one tells me it is my own flesh that is rotting off my back.

My father chooses this moment to remarry. My back is healed and I return to his house and now there are new photos in heavy silver frames. My stepmother wears a watery blue jacket and skirt. Her eyes are huge and dark and her hair is a frizzy triangle of deep red. My father is beside her. She looks like she's won an award. He looks like the runner-up.

My stepmother is from Peru. She has two children from her other husband and a voice like scratched metal. She does not take her eyes off my father. She has money and a big house, which is where he lives now. Her children are teenagers. They go to boarding school and when they come home they are glazed and polite but they do not want to play and they do not want me in their rooms. My stepmother comes to fetch me from my mother's flat. She arrives in her sleek pale blue car. We watch her from our third-floor window. She totters uncertainly on the pavement.

"Come on," says my mother. "She'll never make it up these stairs."

We meet her on the doorstep. My mother smiles, invites her in. My stepmother wafts her away. She does not know my mother yet. She does not know she has nothing to fear, that my mother holds only love and a little suitcase of clean clothes in her hands. My stepmother brushes it away.

"We have clothes for her," she says.

At their house I wear dresses with big collars and matching coats, white tights with no holes in them, and black shiny shoes that scuff if you trip. My stepmother brings me fat dolls from America and a Lego set that lights up. She brings me back clothes from Miami, a place that sounds like an exotic cat, frightening things I don't understand but that I pretend to love— neon swimsuits made of toweling, sweatshirts with detachable hoods and words scribbled on the chest in electric colors. My mother smiles and stuffs them back in my suitcase.

"Wear this when you are with them," my mother says.

I am seven. My father picks me up from school. He never picks me up. He often takes me to school, always late, in his tight white car where only the two of us can fit. He kisses me and threatens to walk me inside with his blue pajamas sticking out of his soft camel coat. But he never picks me up.

Someone must have told me he was coming. Someone must have told me she was coming. But I do not remember that. He is in the big car. He leans around as I run toward him, his elbow on the headrest, his head turned back to me smiling. I hold my red beret so it will not fly off my head. I fling open the back door. There is already someone in the backseat. There is a small boy curled up against the far window. He is hunched into himself like a curved brown animal. He has the shortest hair I have ever seen and he is staring at me.

"This is your new sister, my love. Give her a kiss."

Everything feels far away and upside down. I never disobey my father. I slip my body inside the car and lean across the backseat. I travel the vast distance between us to kiss the boy who is actually a girl on her little brown cheek. She scrambles back farther against the window and raises her hand between us and claws at my face with her fingers. My cheek blooms and stings. I sit back, astonished, holding my face. I do not understand. This is not how it goes. I do not know anyone who tells the truth like this, with their whole body. I do not want a sister but I do not know that I do not want a sister because I am not allowed to know this. I am being kind, which is what my mother is, and this is not how kind goes. Kind is what you are even when you don't feel like it. I open a car door and now I have a sister. I have a sister who does not want me. My father rubs my face. He talks all the way home. We sit, all of us, in our separate corners of the car, watching the tall white buildings turn into parks, into streets, into a world none of us has ever known before.

My adopted sister came from the jungles of Paraguay. My father visited a sugar plantation for work and next door there was an orphanage. He asked to visit it and was introduced to a young girl whose parents had died in a car crash and he brought her home as a present for my stepmother. This is the story I am told. This is the story I tell for years until I hear myself tell it one day, and I realize there was no car crash. There was only a terrified teenager too young to imagine raising a daughter. There was no spontaneous adoption, there was my stepmother, too old to conceive, craving a baby with her husband. There were lawyers, interviews, and the slow crawl of bureaucratic time.

My adopted sister lives with my father and his wife all the time. I visit them on weekends. At the beginning it feels like she is my guest. But soon it feels like I am hers. Our closet sways with twin dresses, one slightly smaller than the other. I have blue eyes and a round face, hair the color of toffee and a belly like a planet. My adopted sister has dark brown eyes and all her body is sticks. We are dressed identically but carry our private worlds within us. I play with her, gesturing to toys, to books. She doesn't speak English. She doesn't speak Spanish. She speaks the language of the jungle. She watches me, always. She loves me because she watches me and I let her and I love her because I do not know what else to do although there is a feather in my throat when I see my father hold her. She waits for me to visit at weekends. She asks to come to my house and see where I live all week. My mother, because she is my mother, invites my adopted sister to tea, to stay the night, holds her in her lap to read to her.

There is a photograph of us, my adopted sister and I, side

by side in the painted-jungle bedroom. I am sitting in bed, reading. I am smiling at the camera, hair and eyes shiny. Beside me, in a matching bed, in a matching nightgown, sits my adopted sister, holding a matching book. She is not looking at the camera. She is looking at me. Her book is upside down.

I am pregnant with my second child. We spend nine months preparing my daughter for the birth of her brother. We buy her a baby doll to love and dress and bathe. She drags it around by its foot. She climbs into the new baby's empty crib every day, lays in it, rolling around in it, listening to it, mapping it. She rests her head on my belly, kisses it. She kisses the bomb that will reconfigure her world. It feels like treachery. We are giving her the greatest gift, we tell ourselves.

My son picks his own birthday even though we have chosen one for him. He rumbles his arrival and is pulled from my belly a few weeks before the date we have picked, finding us all lightly unprepared. My husband and I drive to the hospital at dawn leaving our oblivious sleeping daughter with our cleaning lady. My son arrives insistently but without drama and a few hours later my husband returns home to shower and scoop up our daughter to bring her to the hospital.

I lie in my hospital bed waiting. I have soaked in my new son all morning but now I must share him. I hear her footsteps in the hospital corridor. I hear my husband help her with the heavy door. She is a tangle of blond sweat and her thumb is a plum in her mouth. She widens to see me and flings her car-hot body on mine. She strokes the back of her own neck. The baby sleeps in his plastic box by the window. She does not see him yet. She only breathes me. I clamber to my feet and wheel the box to the bed. She stands on the bed, peers in. She rocks from foot to foot, thumb in her mouth, holding her nape, stroking it over and over. She is hectic, she is giddy, she wants to hold him. We only watch her, the baby ignored, smug in his muslin wrap, unassailable. We hold her back, we smile at her enthusiasm. She is drunk with power. She dances for us, she sings, she waits for us to shush her. She tries to rock the baby but the baby sleeps on. I grow tired, she grows tired. It is time for them to leave. She climbs up beside me. She thinks I am coming with them. I shake my head, hand her to my husband. She clings to my neck like a noose. We have not prepared her for this.

She does not understand why I am staying. She does not know why the baby can have me and she cannot. She is blindsided. My husband carries her sobbing from the room. She struggles from his arms as he shepherds her across the maternity ward to the elevator. The elevator arrives but she will not get in, will not leave her mother alone with that baby. He nudges her in, she will not move. He steps past her, into the elevator, holding open the doors, inviting her to follow him in. But hospital doors will not be held. The doors close on their terrified faces and she is left screaming, alone on the maternity floor, and he is swept sickened down to the ground floor. He presses every button, stops at interminable floors, escapes, tears up staircases to find her. He finds her, two years old in a corridor of concerned nurses, undone by the father who has abandoned her in a hospital, by the mother who has betrayed her with another, by the white bundle that never spoke or moved and changed everything.

My husband calls me on the speakerphone from the car. He sounds more exhausted than I feel. I hear my daughter sobbing and raging behind him. My son tugs at my breast and my heart sags. I cannot reach her. I cannot nuzzle her sweaty head. So I start to sing. I am not a singer. I sing anyway. I sing every nursery song I have ever known. I sing Christmas carols, I sing hymns, I sing anything I know the words to. I sing her through the city, along the freeway, the ocean with the dying light licking the hills and the far dark line of the sky against the sea, up the winding hill, and down the path to our home. I sing her into submission, into sleep, into her new life.

At my father's house, we play monster at bedtime. First, we read my favorite book, about the boy who is sent to bed with no supper, which is a terrible punishment, and my father leans over me and kisses me and says good night and kisses me again and closes the door. I lie in the dark, electric, fizzing, knowing, waiting. I hear the door click. A crack of light. Then darkness again. Silence holds me. I hold my breath. The room is darker than a jungle. I can see nothing. But I know he is circling. He is crawling around my bed like a jaguar. He is stealth and I am trembling. I wait. I know I must wait. But I cannot bear to wait. I want to explode with the waiting.

I call his name.

No reply. Again, I say his name. Nothing. No breathing. Not even mine. The darkness is rough. I breathe one teaspoon at a time. A snarl, a grab, shrieking. My ankle is ripped from the covers. I cannot tell what is my voice and what is his. I am terrified. The monster strikes again, grabbing my other foot, on the other side of the bed now. I am sobbing, laughing, dying, alive. The light turns on. My father stands over me. He looks at me perplexed.

"A monster came!" I tell him.

"No," he says, "impossible. I was outside your door the whole time."

And we laugh and he kisses me good night for real this time and he leaves. He kisses my adopted sister too. She loves monster even more than I do. I notice he does not grab her as often but I never mention it. Once, in his bathroom, when he is shaving and I am perched on the sink facing him, watching his face emerge from the white foam, he whispers to me, "I love you the most because you're mine."

And I know I am not meant to know this, that he has given me a secret thing that can hurt, a monster that will bite you in the dark.

He was not mine. He was not only mine. I shared him with many women. My husband tells me I got more of him than anyone. It never felt like enough. He left daughters littered behind him like a careless man might leave expensive raincoats.

Home

I AM TWENTY-SIX. I arrive in the city with a job, some money, but no friends. I move into a low white apartment with a little fireplace and old wooden floorboards and a buckling courtyard at the back with an avocado tree bursting through it. I buy my fruit at the farmers market, walk it home to ripen it on the sunlit windowsill. I take a bath and hear a thud. Dripping bathwater, I find a peach glistening, lightly gnawed, rolling on the kitchen floor. At night I hear noises in the walls. Rats, I tell my landlady. Fruit rats she assures me, as though the fruit made them tolerable, healthy even. Across the courtyard lives the son of a famous actor. He sleeps till the afternoon, is unfailingly polite, and has a girlfriend who cannot meet my eyes. One morning I hear cries. I stuff the pillow over my head. I still hear them. I hear breaking glass. I hear the girlfriend's voice grow shrill, a scream, a breaking sound. I stand at his door before I know my feet have moved. I am banging at his door. I have no idea what I am going to say.

Silence.

He comes to the door. He has no shirt on, he is slick with

sweat, his skin is gray as an unripe avocado. I look past him. The girl hovers in a doorway, swaying, slender, head shaking.

"Are you okay?" I ask her.

She nods.

He apologizes for waking me. I do not look at him. I look at her. She stares at the floor.

"Tell me you are okay."

She looks at me.

"I am okay," she whispers.

He turns back at her and then to me.

"Sorry," he says. "I'm so sorry."

I look beyond him, deep into the darkness of that corridor. She has turned away.

I walk back to my apartment. I hold my hands in front of me. They are shaking. Vermin I can live alongside, but not violence. I move out. I find a new house, a pale yellow one, in the canyons, leafed with eucalyptus, nooked in the hillside, with an even bigger fireplace and wider-planked oak floors and a Dutch door I lean out of, smoking. An old hunting lodge from the twenties. It has built-in bookcases and a drop-down desk. Squirrels wake me. I send to England for my books. I eat noodles so I can pay my rent. I borrow money. My coffee table is a single plank that rests on six volumes of the *Oxford English Dictionary*. The other six fill the shelves, and beside them, my plays, my books, my recipes. I read in the paper that the famous actor's son has gone to jail. I throw dinners and baby showers.

The house fills and empties like a rock pool. It is mine. It is my home.

I am offered a job on a tropical island. It will take years to film. I do not want to go. I do not want to move again. I do not want to give up this world that I have so carefully assembled, friend by friend. No one understands. Actors move. We are carney folk. We change clothes, hair, accents, sizes, names, and location. I refuse. I do not accept this part of the job. I want to root myself where I am. I want to be still. I want to be the place where people gather. I want to hold myself together because I know how easily we are scattered and lost. I take a smaller part on the show, I fly back and forth to the island. I host Thanksgivings and brunches, date the wrong men, and swing from my Dutch door, smoking.

These days I rarely leave town for work. I blame my children. But it is not my children. I do not want to leave the home I have made for myself. I do not want to uproot what has taken so long to take seed. I do a job that allows me to be someone else. It allows me to use a voice that is resentful, disobedient, outspoken, angry, cruel. This is not a voice my life has allowed for. I do a job that I chose without knowing what I was choosing. I am twenty when I decide this is what I must do, can only do. I think I am choosing adventure, but actually I am choosing to behave in all the ways that were forbidden me as a child for fear of losing someone I love. My job allows me to travel terrain that was unmapped in the topography of my childhood. There is enough new territory for me to chart without leaving home as well.

I am six and seven and eight. I visit my father in London on the weekends. He lives with my stepmother and her voice like rust. I am happiest in the basement, which is my father's office. There is a leather sofa that you slide off when you sit on it but no one sits on it. There is a huge tiger facing sideways on one wall and in front of it a fax machine that unspools paper sticky with black ink, and a phone with lights to call every room in the house. I call all the rooms, always. My father has a sauna in his basement. We wrap ourselves in towels and go in together. I ladle water on the hot coals. We steam and hiss together. I flee, and wait, faithful as a spaniel, for him to emerge, gasping. There is a cart with whiskey on it and glasses. My father asks me to lay my two fingers on their side and hold them up to the splintered light of the glass. I must pour the whiskey up to the second finger and bring it to him. I do not spill a drop. I sit on his lap while he calls people and laughs. He holds me close, we are damp, hot, inseparable.

My bedroom is as far from his office as you can get. It is on the fourth floor. To get there you must pass the navy-blue kitchen where my father, sleep mask pushed up on his forehead, fries fish fingers for me on Saturday mornings and leaves me with a pool of ketchup for dipping and all the cartoons.

You must tiptoe past his bedroom where you must always knock because my stepmother is always sleeping. You must climb past the rooms with sofas and silver frames and so many silent china frogs. You must not go into the one where the television is hiding behind a frill beneath a table. Grace Kelly lives in that television and you may watch her once the cartoons are done. You may press Play and watch her again and again and press your nose up so close to the screen and breathe on her as she lies in a white dress in her boat with her arms outstretched and her long white fingers dangling in the water.

This is the room where Grace Kelly lives but also your shame. This is the room where ballet happens. The teacher is slender and soft. The teacher holds her hands in front of her and she sees a basket of flowers, a cloud, a dream. You hold out your hands and there are only hands with ketchup on them. The elastic digs into your thighs and the pink leotard is too tight. Your adopted sister looks like a sweet pea, swaying. You look like an Easter egg. Now the teacher teaches a dance from Peru. For it we must wear skirts that billow like sails. We must hold them in one hand and wave a handkerchief in the other. We must dip and sway like a leaf like a butterfly like a sunbeam but I am a boat with a leak and I cannot. I drown. My stepmother tells me I am not trying hard enough. My adopted sister sucks her fingers. She is a butterfly inside a sunbeam. I am waterlogged. We show my father what we have learned. I am trapped in a bottle. I must not let him see my shame. I bob and duck. I watch him hide a smile. I hate him. I love him. I want him to rescue me. He claps loudly, stretches his legs, and leaves.

We must take photographs in our costumes so everyone can see. The photographer comes. He unfurls a backdrop of cloudy pinks and purples. It looks like a bruise. My stepmother brushes our hair till it hurts and shines. We have new dresses for these photos. Mine is a bright embroidered dress that Peruvian ladies wear. It is red and black and stretches itchy across my chest. There are tiny mirrors in the skirt. It smells like a sack. My face is pale and rigidly smiling beneath the wide flat-topped hat. It is the kind of hat Peruvian women wear to carry things down a precipice. But I have nothing that needs carrying, I am dancing in a drawing room in Kensington knowing everything is wrong and that there is no one to tell it to. I am trapped in a photograph in the national dress of Peru.

Next to this room is my father's dressing room. You may go in here if he is with you. You may press the flat doors that have no handles and they open smooth with a soft sigh to reveal a wall of tiny glass shelves, each one lit, each one holding a shirt, so soft, with perfect creases in them, with his initials sewn in tiny letters on the cuffs. Like dolls' clothes, colors so creamy. In the morning I dress him. He picks his suit, and I pull each quiet shelf out in turn, until I find the shirt that will be exactly the right one. I lay it next to the suit. Next the tie, chosen from the wall of bright cascading ribbons of color, racing horses, soaring birds, tiny tigers, and a horse and carriage on the back of every one. Then the handkerchief, not matching, never matching because that is not how we do it. We lay them out on the table and together we go up one more flight to his bathroom.

It is a room so full of steam I cannot tell you its color. Wet walls and dark wood and gold taps. I sit on the sink. He sprays shaving foam on his face, hands it to me. I spray mine. We look at our white faces in the mirror. He arches his cheek and pulls his blade along it, freeing his face. I take the wrong end of my toothbrush and scrape my cheeks clean, mirroring his movements. Suds drip. I make no noise. I must not distract him so he does not hurt himself and make his face bleed and then he will growl and stick a tiny piece of tissue on his face. This room takes hours. He will take me to school when he is ready. I am already late. My stomach is tight but he will be angry if I tell him, so I sit on the sink, satchel sticky with suds, waiting.

At the very top of my father's house is my room. The curtains match the wallpaper match the bedspreads. It is like being trapped in a jungle. A huge Barbie house sits in one corner. It has an elevator you draw up with a weighted string and a too-big horse that sits outside chewing painted grass. Ken gets stuck in the elevator but if you yank it you can drag him up to the top floor, which is also where the bedrooms are. My father's parents come to visit from Argentina and bring me a suitcase full of inflatable dollhouse furniture. It is not designed for Barbie, it is meant for another kind of doll, and it is all too big.

The empty rooms are stuffed with squeaky sofas that Barbie slides off and a refrigerator that you can't open. I play with her in the folds of the heavy flocked curtains so she can be jungle Barbie. There is a rocking horse with real fur and a leather saddle. Leather means you must not sit on it when you are wet and naked after the bath or you will leave a heart-shaped mark on it that you think is beautiful except that your stepmother does not think so and will slap your wet behind and then it is her turn to leave a mark but this one has fingerprints so that when you go home, and have another bath, your mother sees, asks, What is this? And you tell her and after that your stepmother does not touch your naked body ever again.

This house is my home, my other home. This is where I come until one day when I am eight and it is sold and then they are gone.

There are so many places that my father lives after that. Apartments, borrowed, leased, and owned; offices with sofa beds; hotel rooms, high-rises, houses. None of them has a room that is mine. I am welcome, always welcome, but never home.

Peru

I READ AND READ AND READ. I cannot read enough. There are not enough books for my hunger, I cannot keep up with myself. I read beyond my years, deep into the years ahead. I am unreachable in my book. I am alone and in company. No one asks you what you're doing with a book in your hand. No one asks you if you're okay. No one asks you anything at all.

I am eight. England and Argentina go to war over some tiny islands that no one has ever heard of. In assembly, in our striped dresses, shivering in the cold spring sunlight, we pray for the English soldiers in their fight against the Argentines. I come home, bury myself in my mother's lap, confide that I think I may have prayed for someone to kill my father. My father has never fought a day in his life but my prayer feels like a betrayal. My mother goes to see the headmistress. The next day, and every day thereafter, we pray for both the English and the Argentine soldiers. No one in London wants to do business with an Argentine. For this, and other reasons, my father and his wife move to Lima, Peru, where she is from.

Empty space. I do not remember them leaving. I do not

remember the house being packed up, my bedroom crated, my clothes folded, the axis of my life upended. I remember no longer seeing my father on the weekends, no longer traveling with him to European ski slopes, beaches, hotels. I remember him no longer picking me up from school, and I remember him no longer swerving through dark streets with the stars in the cold sky and me warm, wrapped in a duvet, in the back of his open-topped car to return me to my mother's on a Sunday night. I remember wondering if he would forget about me or if I did something to make him leave. I remember waiting for him to call and tell me when he was coming back for me. I remember all the promises to visit and how often he broke them.

The house in Lima has a pool and a blazing white wall all the way around it and a garden with no grass but only cement and an avocado tree that drops leaves like canoes into the water. My father lazes on a lilo, slim as a lizard, with my sister on his lap, clinging like an organ-grinder's monkey. She eyes me implacably, knowing she has won. She is his now, and I am the interloper.

I am given a friend who is not my friend but the daughter of someone my stepmother knows. She is dark, intense, with a blackbird's wing of hair that swoops in front of her face. She is the daughter of the most famous writer in Peru. She is sullen. My father is not a famous writer and I worry that this is the problem between us. I don't speak enough Spanish and she speaks no English but no one seems to have thought of this. We are left in the backyard. My adopted sister is at school and now I miss her. The girl with black hair walks carefully heel to toe all the way around the edge of the pool. I watch her. I ask her if she'd like a snack. She does not reply. I go inside. I watch her from the kitchen, still balancing heel, toe, heel, toe all the way around the pool's edge, back and forth. Her lips are moving, her arms outstretched. She never looks up. Her house-keeper comes to collect her and she leaves without saying good-bye. At dinner my stepmother wants to know how the playdate went.

"She was nice," I offer helplessly.

"Good," says my stepmother.

The girl never comes back to play.

I visit Lima again and now the house is gone and now we live in two apartments that are on top of each other. If I want to see my father, I have to take the elevator. My adopted sister and I live in the lower apartment with the dogs and the married couple who cook and clean for my stepmother. William and Negrita are the dogs' names. They are low and pointy. I don't remember the married couple's names. I sit in the white tiled kitchen on a Formica stool and spoon bowlfuls of earthy brown lentils and rice into my mouth. After lunch we may go upstairs. I push the gold button in the elevator because my adopted sister lives there so she always gets to. We press ourselves up

51

against the plate-glass windows and breathe on them, making fog inside to match the rolling fog outside that drenches the oceanfront view. We wait for the afternoons when we will be taken to the club. There is a pool there, and a beach with waves that will knock you inside out and upside down and spit you back out on the beach like a peach pit. The beach is dotted with parasols made of dried palm fronds, and if you sit at a white plastic table they will bring you panqueques con dulce de leche, which are crepes filled with soft buttery caramel and then sprinkled with sugar, and they make my tongue ooze and I want all of them, there are never enough of them to make me stop wanting them. My father meets us there after work and he will let me order one more. Sometimes. Other times he will shake his head and click his tongue and flick the swimsuit elastic on my soft thighs. "No more, my love. You don't want a fat tummy." In his mouth, it rhymes with Mommy.

It is Christmas and we are dressed in matching smocked dresses but mine is blue for my eyes and hers is pale pink. There are more parcels than I have ever seen under the tree and I know to light my eyes up and tumble from one to the next and I miss my mother so much. The sash digs into my waist and I cannot breathe but I reach for another and another and another as though they were the oozing caramel pancakes and the sweetness could stuff the missing out of me. I take my dress off that night and find the fine imprint of the smocking spider-webbed across my chest.

We fly to a lagoon in Peru that my stepmother owns. We cannot take many things because they are too heavy for the plane. The landing strip looks like a forehead in the jungle. It is dark and full of rustling and men with torches help us out of the plane and toward jeeps parked beneath noisy trees. We slash through the darkness, bumping, in a blackness full of sounds. I hear water. We bump stop. We climb into canoes that tilt and sway and strange hands reach out to hold me, settle me. I sit, clutching my backpack, feeling the edges of my books digging into my thighs, tin cans pressing into my back. My father's voice ahead. My stepmother calm, reassuring. We lurch and then smooth onto the dark water. Lapping, hissing from the shore. Houses with thatched roofs that cling to the edges of the water. One house sticks out of the water on stilts. It looks like Baba Yaga's hut. I worry it will walk toward us, that there will be a witch inside it. Men crunch our boats onto the shore and we step out and sway-walk toward the thatched houses. I share a hut with my adopted sister. Our beds are low with nets spread over them. We undress in the dark, a dim flashlight between us that we have promised to conserve. I gesture to her to switch it off. We have been apart for so long we no longer speak each other's languages. I climb beneath her white netting and we lie together shrouded and listen to the noises of the jungle.

There are other families here, friends of my stepmother. The famous writer and his daughter are here. We play cards hatefully in the Baba Yaga hut. My adopted sister watches, teeth small and white, misshapen like the tiny pearls my step-mother's son finds when he dives in the lagoon. She laughs at everything I do. There is nothing fresh to eat here but fish. I drink only the sweet milk from tins. My father brings crates of this milk to trade with the men who walk out of the jungle. I drip it onto cereal. Sticky white drops that make a thick slurry. The cornflakes drown in sweetness. I have a headache all the time. I sweat and read and finish my books too soon. My blue shorts grow tight but I smile so no one will notice. No one does. I want to call my mother but there is no way to call from the jungle. I miss milk. I wait to go home. The adults laugh inside their own language and a haze of cigarette smoke.

I am ten. We go to the capital city of the Incas, my father, his wife, my adopted sister, and I. It is higher than I have ever been. We wear wool ponchos and cowboy hats and my stomach turns and churns from being so high in the clouds and from pressing my ear to the thin hotel walls to overhear their fights. My stepmother's voice is as scratchy as the ponchos. I hear it crack and sob through the wall. The city is thin-aired with narrow streets and thick with sellers pressing brightly woven dolls, key chains, T-shirts into my small white hands.

We go higher still, to where the air feels so thin you could slash it with your fingernail. It feels like the membrane of an eyeball. We take the zigzag train up the mountain. It lurches back and forth, a slow concertina carved into sheer rock. It is inexorable, endless. I cling to the carriage to make it cling to the mountain. It is cold and bright and my lungs and eyes burn. There is nothing to see but mist. We are clutching an invisible mountain wrapped in a cobweb. My father wears his favorite jacket, the puffy one with the sew-on patches from his race-car days. It rustles when he talks. He is eager, clutching my adopted sister in his lap. He tells us the story of a fabled city to which the Incas fled from the Spanish invaders, lost to history for centuries until one man, an American explorer, determined to find it, beat back the jungle, and threaded a path through the needle-top mountains to the summit, where he stumbled on an entire silent city. This is a story I know, because there is always a maiden who has slept for a hundred years and always a knight who must force his way through the forest to find her. I cannot wait to see the castle and perhaps there will be a princess there, one that everyone else overlooked. This thought comforts me as I bite back the tides of nausea and the pressure that drums in my temples. My adopted sister wails and lies down in her mother's lap. I sit up and look out and dig my fingernails into my palms to stop from crying out. My father nods approvingly. I taste bile in my mouth as we climb higher and higher but there is no turning back. My stepmother watches him. The mist drains into the bowl of the Andes. We are here. We are here. We arrive at the top, tumble out, unsteady. We stagger to the ticket booth on uneven feet. I am eager, desperate to prove to my father that I am not troubled by the altitude, and to see for myself what this lost city looks like. I follow my father, clicking his heels, hungry for Inca gold.

We step through the ticket booth and out into the damp sunlight. My father stops, breathes out, and places his hand on my shoulder. I frown. I look where he looks. There are no castles here. There are no spires, no vaulted windows, no locked doors, no cellars, no attics, no secret staircases veined with thorny vines. There is only a vast silent flatness with gray stones slung in long low walls. They thread the plateau, rising and falling. There are arches and terraces, rows and rows of small enclosures, walls rising and falling, climbing hilltops and cresting into a lookout, an altar, a temple. It seems bereft. An abandoned honeycomb. Strange lidless boxes of air wide open to the sky above. The citadel is nestled in green peaks that needle the clouds and the tight gray stones that lay quietly like obedience. I sigh in disappointment and the longing to throw up and lie down. My father squeezes my shoulder.

"I knew you'd love it."

We spend the day picking through the pathways, the temperature rising, the roar of a river below, the sound of our guide and others like him naming our way through the ruins. Bathhouse, jail, tomb, drain, sentry, temple of the sun, vending machine. We peel off layers, we drink warm sticky drinks, we thread our way through ancient stones and roofless temples to the edge of everything under an aching sky. I am frightened of the edges, of the altars and the drops and the birds arcing overhead. My father moves quickly, asking questions, sharing answers with me, frowning to see my adopted sister sitting, resting in the shade of an archway, her face leaning against the stone, my stepmother shaking her head. Eventually, when the mind can hold no more, it is time for us to leave. We gather in the waiting room for the funicular to take us back down the mountain. It is cool in here, and the long day is ending. We dress quietly and here my father realizes he has lost his jacket. He asks us all in turn if we have it. We shake our heads. He pats himself down as though he has hidden it on his own body. He asks my stepmother why she does not have it. He insists he gave it to her to carry, perhaps even to wear. His lips go white. His eyes are small and black like Inca beads. I have never seen him like this. She was carrying it, she was in charge of it, how could she have dropped it, how could she have mislaid something so precious. The room grows smaller as he rages until he can barely fit in it any more and he bursts away. We sit. We wait. I cannot look at my stepmother. I cannot believe she could lose something so precious. I cannot believe she would not take better care of my father's love.

My stepmother slips on her dark glasses. My adopted sister dozes in her mother's lap. I pull out my book. I read *Uncle Tom's Cabin* at the top of Machu Picchu. There is a photo of me reading it. I am wearing a brown poncho and a cowboy hat. I am sitting cross-legged. I read about escape and the white man's dominion over brown bodies while sitting on the top of a mountain to which, centuries earlier, more brown bodies fled to escape the white man's fist. But I know none of this. I only know how to plunge my pain like a hot blade into the cool depths of the written page. I know how to submerge and disappear and every book I ever read has opened its pages to me with the promise that it will hold me, it will never abandon me, it will never let me go.

My father returns empty-handed. He does not speak to anyone for the rest of the evening. In silence we ride down that mountain, slide back to the hotel, to our rooms. He holds silence like a lost fortress and we wander around his ruin.

Years later, on a hot balcony overlooking a snake of traffic winding into Buenos Aires, I ask him about the jacket he lost at the top of the Andes. He looks thoughtful. He has forgotten about it. He tells me that he had cocaine in the pocket. He tells me he loved the jacket, with all its history, but he was more worried he'd lost his stash. He snorts, flicks his joint over the balcony, and stretches his back.

I am ten. It is my last night in Lima. My father no longer lives with my stepmother. He has his own apartment now. It is dim and made of wood and there is a black leather chair that swivels and tilts. He makes us hot dogs and rice and cheese, and he teaches me backgammon. I lose and lose and lose and he laughs at my tight face and I hate him. I am leaving the next morning and I cannot speak. I do not know when I will see him again and I know I must not ask him because it will make him stop laughing and he will turn his head away from me. I sleep on the sofa, balled up like a fist.

The next morning he walks me onto the plane, buckles me into my seat, tucks a satchel in my lap, and hands me a thick old hardback book with gold writing on the spine. I recognize it from his bookshelf.

"Don't look up till you get there," he says.

He kisses me, smiles at the air hostess, who blooms, and walks off the plane. I watch him leave and now my eyes and the root of my tongue hurt but I must not feel them, because now I am going home to my mother whom I have missed without words but with my bones. The airplane lady puts a hand on my shoulder. I cannot feel it. I watch him walk tall across the tarmac. I keep my bag in my lap. I hold it like a bear. And then I begin to read. I read with the book propped up against the seat back while I eat everything that is put in front of me. Later, I stop to go to the bathroom where I pull out the little bag he has tucked in there for me. It is pale yellow and has an orange Inca symbol on it. Inside is a comb, a washcloth, a little mirror, and a tiny plastic rectangular box. I open it and there is a toothbrush head and the handle tucked beside it and wedged in between the smallest toothpaste I have ever seen.

I wedge my thick fingers in to get at it and then notice the tiny note that is stuck to the inside of the box. It is a piece of paper, cut to size, with a smiling-sun face and the word "SMILE" in my father's writing. I lean my head against the wall of the plane and I cry till my heart is dry. I will not use the toothbrush in case I accidentally drop water on the note so I carefully replace it, wash my mouth out with water, rinse my red face, and walk back to my seat. The book is the true story of a man who makes a raft of balsa wood and sails from Peru to Polynesia to prove that centuries earlier other men had done this. I weep as I read, pushing the words down inside me, filling my well with stones. I finish the book by the time I land. It sits by my desk as I type this.

I return from these trips back to the arms of my mother. I have no words for what these trips have actually been like. I share what I know will please, the places traveled, lessons learned, the myths. I hold them up like seed pearls dredged from the bottom of a dark lagoon. I have no way to say, I missed you, I ached for you, and now I am here I miss him, and where must I stuff this missing now. I must protect them all from the ferocity of my feelings. So I stuff the missing into my belly and lecture anyone who will listen about the lost city of the Incas and the seafarers of Easter Island.

Catamaran

I AM NINE. Now that my father lives in Peru I have to fly alone to visit him. He arranges to meet me halfway. I fly alone to an island in the Caribbean. I carry a satchel packed with books, a name tag around my neck, and I stare at the floor so I won't cry as my mother waves goodbye to me from the jetway. I arrive to a halo of wet heat, my father in an open-top jeep and an open-necked shirt. He wears a long gold chain I have not seen before. A little amulet hangs from it. His witch doctor gave it to him, he tells me. A brujo. He must never take it off. We stay in a hotel that sits on pink sand. We have two days together and I feel the hours trickling like pink sand through my hands. I wear the striped swimsuit my stepmother gave me. I must be so good because this is so fun and I do not have to share him with anyone here. He rents a catamaran for the day and we take it out. I ask if he has sailed one before. He assures me he has. I know immediately that he has not. We sail away from the island. We snorkel. The water is clear, the colors brilliant. He dives down deep, cuts me a piece of bright coral with his penknife. He surfaces with it, glistening. We both know this is not allowed. The coral turns pale in my lap. An island breeze picks up. The wind turns dark. I ask to go back. He sits on one edge of the catamaran, hauling on a rope. The catamaran tilts on its side. I think this is not how it is supposed to go. One hull yawns out of the water. The sail stiffens, seizes. We slice through the water. We are perpendicular to the ocean, only one hull anchors us, the other drips white against the darkening sky. I cling to the hull that is still in the water as we bounce and skim across the waves, the sail taut, salt spray slathering us. We are windsurfing a catamaran on its side. There are no other boats still in the bay. I yell at my father. I ask if this is how it is supposed to be sailed.

"Of course!" he yells back. His knuckles are white. The little amulet bounces on his slick chest. I can tell he is angry. I clutch the coral to my life vest.

We scud and skid our way onto the shore, tumble onto the ragged beach. The vendor wades out to meet us, shaking his head, clucking his tongue, gesturing furiously. My father brushes him off. He hurries me up the beach back to the hotel, laughing. That night he drinks three whiskeys and his eyes glitter. I tell him how much fun I had. And I did. And I did not. For years afterward whenever I see people in catamarans sailing smoothly, both hulls in the water, I think that those people are doing it wrong. I wait for them to tilt up on one edge, to skim their backs to their ocean like we did. I pity them and their smooth even sail. But deeper still, I know my father is the one doing it wrong.

Salt

MY PARENTS GO to Paris for their honeymoon. She is eighteen, a stalk of new corn in the sunlight. He is twenty-six and looks like a French movie star. They fly to Paris on tickets my grandfather gives them and stay in a little hotel no one can remember the name of. They spend five days there. There is one photo of my mother smoking, looking into the distance. The river is behind her. She looks so private, lost in herself. It is the opposite of the nakedness I associate with a honeymoon. I ask her about the photograph. We are locked in our houses on opposite sides of the world. There is time to speak and nothing but time because the world has stopped. We have only closeness now that everything else has been stripped from us. I ask questions about how my parents met, their courtship, their wedding, their honeymoon. She speaks, I listen, but I know these stories. These are the authorized versions. What I want has yet to be spoken. She is dizzying, dazzling in her recall of facts, of details. I wait.

I ask her how she felt on her honeymoon. She falters. I nudge my way in. She closes her eyes. I can hear her. She is lying down on the bed she has shared with my stepfather for the last thirty-five years. I hear her drop inside the well of herself. I feel her listen for the truth. (Truth, in my family, is the outspoken drunk we reluctantly invite for Christmas, the relative we know we should love but whom no one wants to talk to.) I watch her trapped between the desire to protect herself and the longing to share what has not been shared before.

"Our honeymoon was hard," she says. "We fought from the moment we arrived."

I ask her why.

"He had no money," she says.

I ask her what she means.

"I mean I paid for our hotel. I paid with the money from my parents. It was my money, my wedding money. My money for starting our new life. I could not believe he had come on his honeymoon and had no way of paying for it. I had never heard of a grown-up having no money. I didn't think it was possible."

She breathes.

"I think it was the beginning of the end."

I am twelve. My father comes to visit me. He brings a girlfriend. She is not my stepmother. I have never met her before. This is a woman who looks like a wolf. She is impatient with him, with us, with life. She wears a long white coat and shivers with cold. They stay for a few days in a flat they have borrowed in a part of London where the museums are. But we never go to a museum. There is no bed for me where they are staying so he picks me up from my mother's in the afternoons after school, and we eat dinner in unfamiliar restaurants.

In the other London, when I am younger, my father and my stepmother and my adopted sister and I go to restaurants on Saturday nights. We go to a new American restaurant where they bring you whole racks of dark spareribs. We sit in wooden booths with dim lights and tie plastic bibs around our necks and everyone smiles as wide as America. Huge food arrives, platters of ribs and baskets of golden steaming onion rings and fries as thick as my thumb. My father and I feast with dark sticky fingers while my stepmother pokes at the watery lettuce and my adopted sister, tiny in the dark corner of the booth, watches us all, learning our ways. We swish our fingers clean in the bowls of warm water with floating lemon slices and disdain dessert for we are full. Other nights we go to the Italian restaurant with its white tablecloths and potted palms, where they escort us always to the same table at the back, pull my chair out for me like a grown-up, and unasked bring us veal Milanese, crisp and glistening, dishes of pillowy white cheese layered with tomato and basil. I come here alone with my father. Here is where I learn to squeeze lemon on fried food, to salt everything before I even taste it, to skip bread, but not always. Here we eat in silence, in love. From my father comes my love of the cured meat, the olive, the potato chip, the caper. Salt is what we share. Salt preserves us, sugar corrupts.

But now, with the wolf lady, everything is different. We go to restaurants I do not know and where the waiters do not know us. Everything feels rushed and unloved. My father is agitated, always in motion. He is impatient with me. He looks to the wolf lady often, for agreement, for consent. I have not seen him ask permission before. She is unreachable.

I have a bank account of my own. It comes with a checkbook with a pale blue cover and the outline of a white bird on the front. I practice writing my signature carefully over and over. Inside the checks bear my name, and the name of the branch, which is the village where my grandmother lives. My grandmother knows the cashier by name, sees her every week. We go together so I can deposit the money I am given on birthdays, at Christmas. I salt it away. I love my checkbook. It makes me feel like I exist in the world. The statements are thrilling. There is my money, existing without me, inviolate, reliable, and utterly mine.

My father drops me back at my mother's. He tells me he needs to borrow my money. He will return it immediately, he says. He just needs it for a week because of a shortfall, a deal is coming, it's all just a matter of timing. He tells me not to tell my mother because there is no need, because it will all be put back in a week. The next morning he and the wolf lady pick me up. We take a cab to a branch of my bank that I do not know. The wolf lady pays for the taxi. She waits outside while we go in. I do not remember signing the check. I do not remember the man behind the glass taking it, calm as a croupier, asking me if I am going to buy something fun with all my money. I do not remember taking the large bright notes and handing them over and watching my father fold them into his pocket as though they are his. I do not remember the wolf lady waiting, outside, smoking among the street pigeons. I remember that he takes all that is mine and he never gives it back and we never speak of it again.

I am six and seven and eight. My father lives in London and works in the futures market. He gambles other people's money in a future where no one lives yet. Life is pristine out there in the unimpeachable future. He makes a fortune. He owns race cars and polo ponies. He buys me dresses I do not need and coats to match. He thrives in this unknown land that is anywhere but now. For his entire life he refuses every job that pays a salary. He works always on commission, stakes his world on a future that he is sure he can predict and control. He fervently believes in a world he alone can see. My father lives like the skydiver he will become. He spends his life leaping into the unknown, defying the laws that govern everyone else, and waiting for the consequences to catch up with him later.

My father is in a hotel room in Marbella. A black nylon bag

sits on the bed. He rolls himself a joint. He is waiting for the phone to ring. He has come here from Peru to buy cocaine. He is going to buy a kilo of it, to sell to friends and to friends of friends. He is not a dealer, he has no time for that. He is a man with money and fast friends who will take this cocaine off his hands. He has been using cocaine for years, a bump here and there, but it creeps up. He is too much in control for anything to be entirely in control of him. But he is always hungry for more of everything, hates to miss an opportunity. He waits. The phone rings.

He drives to the house of the man he must meet with. It is a low white gated house on the beach. Men with guns lean in to his car in the dark. Bougainvillea blooms at the gate. He is waved inside. The living room is dimly lit, cubes of white and the dark sea glittering outside. He sets the nylon bag he is carrying on the floor, takes a seat. The man he has come to see walks in. His hair is parted on the side, shiny, you can see where the teeth of his comb have sleeked his scalp. He wears a short-sleeved shirt, his thick forearms outstretched to my father in greeting. He owns most of the southern coastline. He gestures to someone in the shadows to bring my father his drugs. My father hands him the bag, but the man he came to see waves it away as if it were of no consequence. The exchange is made. The cocaine is in my father's hands. It weighs the same as half a rack of sticky dark ribs. Gunfire crackles outside. They both turn. The doors blast open. Scuffling, bright lights, orders, yelling. New men, men with guns and badges and sirens, are standing over them, immense, black-booted, screaming at them to put their hands on their heads, to lie still, to move away from the fucking bag. The man my father came to see is facedown on the floor. He stares at my father, his cheek pressed into the cold white marble, and my father, heart pounding in his throat, blood raging in his ears, his eyes wide as that dark glittering ocean, stares back.

My father is sentenced to five years in a Spanish jail for intent to distribute. The man my father came to see has been under police surveillance for months. My father is the client who happens to be in the room when the police descend. My father's parents sell the house they built with their own hands to pay for his appeal. They find a doctor who will, for the right sum, testify that my father is an addict and has bought a kilo of cocaine for his own personal use with no intent to supply. My father spends fourteen months in one of the most notorious jails in Europe. I am thirteen. No one tells me where he is.

I am eighteen. I sit on a balcony overlooking Buenos Aires with my father. Lightning splices the sky behind us. I barely notice. He is telling me, for the first and last time, about his experiences in jail. We are high, we pass a joint back and forth. He tells me he was protected, that he was moved to a section for white-collar criminals. He tells me he began a newspaper in the jail. He tells me he took up yoga. He tells me he suffered from stomach acidity and since there was no medication available to him, he simply told his body to stop making acid and it did. He tells me he kept to himself and no one gave him any trouble. I have no idea if he is lying. I have no way of knowing. No one tells a better story. He never speaks of shame, nor of regret. He never speaks of terror or loneliness. He tells me he started a newspaper.

I am thirteen. I am at boarding school. For a year, I receive letters from my father. One a week. They are postmarked Spain. Gossamer-thin blue airmail letters covered in his cramped scrawl. I wonder why he does not visit me, being so close. I wonder, but I know better than to ask because already I know I will not be told the truth. The letters are full of stories and empty of news. He writes about the boy who is sent to bed without any supper and finds himself in a land of monsters. He writes about the boy's travels with his pirate uncle. He writes about invented lands and skirmishes and trades gone awry. At first I read them, glad to hear from my father. I am used to him not knowing how old I am, misjudging my interests, my maturity. I skim them, searching for his promise to visit me. It is never there. I stop reading them, I stuff them in my desk and tell no one. I am ashamed that my father sends me fiction. I am ashamed that I do not know where he is. And I am too ashamed to ask.

I go home, and search my mother's desk. I do not know what I am looking for but I know I must look for something. I find a large brown envelope in a bottom drawer and I take it to her bathroom, the only door that has a lock. The flap is tucked in, not sealed, and I tip the contents on the floor. Photocopies of documents that name my father, legal bills with my grandparents' names on them, depositions translated into English cover the bathroom floor. I read incarcerated, cocaine, sentenced. My wrists pulse and I forget to breathe. I skim what I see and I do not want to see any more. I scoop the papers into the envelope, shake them back into place, tuck the flap in, and tiptoe back to my mother's desk. All these envelopes, the blue and the brown, I push to the bottom of my stomach. I do not want to know what I know. If I ask, I will be lied to. And if I ask again, I will be told the truth, which is worse.

At school we are allowed a single photograph on our dressers. I walk the dormitories studying the photos. They all look identical to me. Mothers and fathers with dogs, girls with brothers, hedges and lawns. I cannot find a frame big enough to hold my family. I have a father and a stepmother, a mother and a stepfather. I have two stepsiblings, a half brother, and an adopted sister. I speak a second language because my mother has made sure I speak it so I will be able to talk to my family, but no one else speaks this language. My mother has done everything she can to give me a normal life. But I am not normal. I am not like these girls. Their fathers come to Sports Day, tall, in blue coats. They yawn during carols and help pack the car. My father is a race-car driver and a polo player. He is incorrigible, I sigh. He travels all the time, I tell the girls. No one has ever met him.

I am in Latin. My teacher, who is Irish and speaks Latin with an Irish lilt, which is how I hear it in my head for the rest of my life, looks up. A prefect stands in the doorway, beckons me out. I follow her to the headmistress's office, wondering what I have done. The corridor is long, hung with dusty tapestries. As I walk, I smell aftershave. It is my father's aftershave. It hangs in the air like faint song. I try not to run because it must be someone else's father, but no one else's father wears this much aftershave and now there he is, impossible in the entrance hall, solid, his head shorn, arms flung wide. I run now and I am in his arms and my face is in his chest which is so strong and so wide and I must never never let him go. The blue-and-brown envelopes flutter in my chest, are airborne.

I start talking. I talk because I know he cannot. He cannot tell me where he has been and I cannot ask. So I start talking. I talk so I do not notice that his black hair is now gray and short like iron filings. I talk so I do not notice the hollows caved in beneath his eyes. I talk so as not to see his beauty drained out of him. I show him around the school as though he were thinking of sending his daughter there. I dazzle him as though he were a prospective parent, not an actual one. I show him squash courts and libraries and locker rooms. I show him everything except myself.

He is exhausted. This is more oxygen than he has had in eighteen months. He has walked out of his cell less than twenty-four hours ago. He has not seen this much green nor so many young women in nearly two years. It is hard to keep up with me. He smiles, weary but willing. I stop everyone, everyone, so I can introduce him, so the girls will see that he exists, he is real, he is mine. I run out of things and people to show. We go into town because just this once we may do that, even though there are lessons, even though it is a weekday. We go to the food store that is luxurious, the one my family uses only for special occasions and treats. My mother, who has brought him straight from the airport to me, has taken money from her wallet and handed it to him so he can spend it on me. And my father takes a basket and piles it high with chocolate, cookies, cakes, and candy. He is giddy, jubilant. And I have no words to tell him, remind him that I do not like chocolate. That we do not eat sweet things. That we never have, he and I. I can feel the day ebbing, I can feel the tide of his going. I can feel the rope tighten in my chest and the blue-and-brown envelopes flutter back to where they lay.

I don't remember him leaving. I think my mother picks him up again and drives him back to the airport. I remember him promising to come back to visit me at school (he never does). I remember walking to my dormitory holding a bag of sweetness and tasting only sourness in my mouth. I lie down facing the wall, clutching the bag against my chest, as though I might keep him with me that way. Later that night I share the sugar with my friends, careless of my new wealth. I keep one square of chocolate back, holding it on my tongue, trying to understand the bitterness.

Return

My father stands naked under an overhead fan in a small rented high-rise apartment that his mother has found him on the outskirts of Buenos Aires. He carefully presses the hot iron around the curve of the neck of his one good shirt.

He sits in the waiting room of a school friend's law chambers. He has eleven dollars in his pocket. An orchid shivers beside him. He is ushered in, embraced. There is the framed law degree, the silver photo frames of laughing skiers on snow, on water, the glint of golden cuff links as the friend offers my father coffee, tea, iced water. This is the only friend who still takes my father's calls. The friend is kind but a coffee is all he can offer him. There is no job for him here. My father lives on the cold tip of society's tongue.

My father pours himself a drink from my grandmother's bar cart. He drains one and pours another. My grandmother scatters her questions with her cigarette ash. My father answers what he chooses to, lets her speak about his sisters, the state of the world, soaking himself in her whiskey and the floodlight of her love. He sees no future, hears only the clinking chain of the past.

Gods

MY FATHER'S MOTHER foresees her only son's birth. She is a judge, a woman of legal briefs and hard evidence, not a dreamer. In bed one night, restless and heavy, she dreams that she is sitting at her dining-room table having dinner with her husband. A huge crack opens up in the wall behind him and the picture on the wall tilts. She looks down and feels wetness in her lap. Her water has broken. She wakes astonished. She tells everyone about her dream. Weeks later the biggest earthquake ever to hit Argentina rocks the northern provinces and the aftershocks are felt the length of the nation. In the capital, my grandmother goes into labor. Tens of thousands of people disappear into the earth as my father arrives in the world. The story of my grandmother's dream enters into myth. My family calls it the chronicle of a birth foretold.

It is quite a responsibility to be born in answer to a prophecy in the midst of a cataclysm. It is the story of the arrival of a minor god. My father searches his whole life for ways to live up to the thunderclap that announces his birth.

For years my father wears a little black amulet on a gold

chain around his neck. A black cylinder clad in gold lace that looks like a tribal mask. Small as my thumbnail. It is given to him by a medicine man who treats him and my stepmother for many years. The medicine man attends to the elite of Peru. He was born in extreme poverty and violence, in the slums of Lima, and has been given the gift of sight and of tongues and is very very powerful, my father tells me. I meet him once, briefly. He has black hair that gleams and does not move as he reaches down to shake my hand. His face is dimpled with a thousand pockmarks and I smell his aftershave for a long time after he leaves. I wonder if the scars on his face are from bullets and why his magic cannot cure them.

Lima. The word is wet and salty in my mouth. A city of extremes, of brittle sunlight and clammy fog, of the high white walls of wealth and damp villages of cardboard flanking open drains. A place where Catholicism and black magic coil into each other, sacred and profane enmeshed like conjoined twins sleeping on a mattress. Everyone I know consults a doctor, a priest, and a brujo.

My father wears his amulet for years. But it disappears from his chest when he leaves jail. A man in a blue uniform thrusts at him a manila envelope from beneath a Perspex window. My father takes it, steps into a small adjacent room, and empties the contents onto a table. There is his wallet, worn and light, embellished with the monogram of a French designer. He once traveled with matching bricks of such luggage. His watch, heavy and cool, now loose on his wrist. His sunglasses, a pilot's glasses, tinted green against the sun, and, here, this thin chain of coiled luck. He holds it at arm's length and regards it, lets it fall in the wastepaper basket beside him. Or he leaves it on the table, serpentine on the envelope, to let another decide its fate. Or he picks it up and stuffs it deep in his pocket, ever superstitious, in case maybe the worst is still yet to come.

I am baptized a Catholic, but when I am young and I visit my father on the weekends, we do not go to church. On Sundays we watch movies, eat fried food, and take the small dogs for small walks. My father leaves England and now I spend my weekends with my grandmother. Now I am a Protestant. On Saturdays we drive to her church, a small steepled place of quiet gravestones and discrete pews where everyone knows just where to sit and when to stand. We bring armfuls of flowers that she has cut from her garden, heaping lilacs nodding their heavy purple scent and a fistful of sweet peas I wrench from where they cling to the netting of her tennis court. We empty the stinking vases of last week's water in the sink in the coolness of the sacristy, and since I cannot manage the iron claw of the garden shears I am free to wander while my grandmother snips. I slide along the polished pews, stack the kneelers five high and wobble-kneel on them, pull moss from gravestones, and watch my grandmother's back, her long straight legs in slim blue trousers, her head high, her hands sure on the blades. It is private, this time, it is ours. God hasn't arrived yet. He comes on Sundays when we must go back to church for the service and the vicar is here so now the little side room has wine and God in it. I must stand and not lie down, nor slide nor pick at the moss. I must behave nicely because now God can see.

I go to a boarding school where I attend chapel daily and for an hour on Sundays. Visiting men drone at us from the pulpit. Sometimes I am moved. Mostly I wonder how long till I can next eat. I move among a sea of blue-cloaked young women, lapped by the tides of loneliness, friendship, and appetite.

I make friends with a girl who is one year older. We are the only girls who have divorced parents, who have two Christmases, who have stepparents and extraneous siblings, who know unpredictability like the other girls know their addresses. One summer I go to stay with her at her mother's house. At night her stepbrother takes us out in his jeep. We bump through the top field with the lights off and the roof down, black branches clawing the sky. The stepbrother asks my friend to light him a cigarette and she lights three, handing one back to me, and I take it because I must and in the dark I watch them. I guess we smoke now. I drag the smoke inside me and I scald my throat and hold the cough because if he hears me cough I will die of the shame. He parks the jeep on the ridge and pulls a long gun from under the seat. He turns on the headlights and a hundred rabbits fling themselves like slingshots across the field. I have never seen so many rabbits. Red ember of his cigarette clenched between his teeth, smoke rising, hair short like a star, he grins and shoots the rabbits in the top field in the flood beam of the headlights. I cling to the roll bar and see my friend's white teeth gleam in the dark as she laughs and laughs so he will not shoot us, I think. I am shaking. I inhale more cigarette. I must not die here.

At school, my friend asks me if I will go with her and meet her father one weekend. I am flattered. No one has ever asked my permission to meet their parents. Parents, and their adjuncts, are mandatory, not optional. We take the train to London. She is nervous and excited. She has not seen him for months. She tells me she has to have someone with her when she sees her father. This is the law. She may not see him alone till she is eighteen. I ask why. She shrugs.

"The judge thinks he's dangerous. He's not. He's just crazy."

I nod. I know crazy.

"You don't need to do anything. You can just sit there."

The father is as tall as a tree with a flock of white hair that flutters like seagulls coming in to roost. He wears a dark three-piece suit and speaks like a dictionary. We sit in a café on a busy London street. I am polite, I know how to do this. He is warm, he is welcoming to us both. He asks my friend questions about her life, her friends, her studies. He knows so much about her. I wonder when he will become crazy. I stir my cappuccino and let the father and daughter talk to each other. In the street outside, tourists queue up to visit an exhibition about planets. He glances over at me, then sees what I am looking at. He snorts.

"Look at them queuing up to be crammed full of lies."

I ask him what he means.

The father tells me there never was a moon landing. He tells me the government lied. He tells me the reflection of the angle of the sun in the astronaut's helmet couldn't possibly, because only a fool, and the rock they brought back came from, and it was all filmed in a desert, everyone promised not to tell. He speaks with authority. He is quite calm. He is my father telling me what to do with a double six in backgammon. I look at my friend. She looks at me. They are waiting for me. I open my mouth.

"Wow," I say.

My friend nods, relieved. The father speaks more. His body inclines toward us. He is animated. I listen. I have never heard a man so eager to teach me. I am dazzled. I don't know how to question him because I have never questioned any man ever. To question is to surrender to the disbelief that I have spent my life suspending.

We take the train back to school. My friend is enlivened, grateful that she has someone she can share him with. She is profuse in her praise of how I have conducted myself. I am quiet. Later that night in our dormitory she smuggles herself beside my bed to tell me she has already called her father and he is impressed by me. If I am interested he would like to send me some information about the moon landing, only if I am curious, of course. I do not know how to say, No thank you, this is a craziness I have not trained for, no thank you. I only know how to say, Yes please how kind thank you for having me. I do not know how to say, Is this what a father is?

"Don't tell anyone," she whispers as she slides back to her bed.

A day later a large envelope arrives in my pigeonhole. It is addressed to me, in a script that looks like a monk has written it in a chamber with a quill. Pages fall out. Photocopies, transcripts, images, facts all proving incontrovertibly that no man ever reached the moon. And at the bottom of the envelope, a phone card. A card with a value of twenty pounds so that if I feel so inclined, I can call him and ask him any remaining questions I might have on the subject. Or any subject.

I read everything.

Later that night I call the father. My friend is beside me. I thank him for all the information he sent me. He asks if I read it. I tell him I did. He asks if understood it. I tell him I did. He laughs, approving. He asks what I learned today. I lift my eyebrows at my friend. She nods, encouraging. I tell him I had biology.

"More lies," he says.

My friend and I hold the phone between us. He tells us that evolution is a theory, that it has never been proven, that the human eye could not possibly, that the planet has only been around for so many, that who has ever seen it actually happen. He says he will send us some more on the subject.

This is how it begins.

Fat envelopes bulging with papers. Black script curling my name. Phone cards, stacks of phone cards, cold feet on worn floorboards, waiting for an empty phone, a private corner, searching always for privacy to read the waterfall of facts. As fast as I can read he sends more. I am voracious. I am a good student. I know how to do this. He excavates the ground beneath my feet. He carves away at the moon, the earth, the stars, the animals. Newton, Darwin, Copernicus silently explode in the abyss. He asks me what I think. I am giddy with discovery and the thrill of secret knowledge.

No man in all my life has ever asked me so many questions.

The father immolates my learning as he praises my burning brain. And when it feels like my world has gone and I am clinging to nothing but a hot coal, then, and only then does he hold out his long white arms.

"I am a man of God."

The world is ending imminently. The Sign of the Beast is embedded in every barcode on everything, we are all tagged, we are all doomed, only the one true church will save us. Not the broken one of my father, nor the apostate house of my mother, but the true one, the one from before times. The one where women dress modestly and learn Latin and the study of herbs, the one where rosaries are spoken aloud for hours to mortify the tongue, the one that requires forsaking all others and refusing all falsehood. He will teach us the one true way.

The father's mind is tight, legal, sprung. I am fifteen. I have no answers for this man. I have been led deep into the maze, I have left no trail to find my way out. And maybe this is how a father is supposed to be.

My friend and I skip chapel in the mornings so we can pray together. We stare out the window during our lessons (except Latin) and neglect to hand in our homework. I am diligent in my neglect because diligence is what I know best. I am flooded with the zeal of the initiate and high-minded contempt for the blue-cloaked girls and their childish things. There is no way to reach me where I am. I give away my short skirts. I bury my lip gloss.

I am at home. I must hide all the photocopies somewhere. There is nowhere to hide them at school. I go up to the loft, my old playroom, and haul out a black trunk with my name on it. It smells of lacrosse. I stuff the papers in and go back to my rosary. No boys call that holiday. I leave my room rarely. I attend no parties. I wait for the next term to begin so I can resume my calls, my studies, so my new life can begin again.

I am back at school. I have a blue book that is my catechism. I must learn it by heart. I must call every night for the question and answer. We call separately now, the friend and I, no longer conjoined twins sleeping on a mattress but siblings now, needing separate instruction. We fall behind. He must come in person to tutor us, says the father. He must come late at night when no one will see him.

Our school sits at the base of a steep hill. Halfway up is a large hospital. This is where we will meet. We wait for the lights to be turned out. We wait for the breaths to lengthen and quieten. We dress in tracksuits pulled over pajamas. We haul ourselves over a windowsill, tiptoe along a battlement, cling to a trellis, and loop our bodies over the wall. We are in the town. The traffic screams. Faces low into the dark we hike up the hill to the car park of the hospital. He sits in his car waiting for us. We burst in, freezing. He turns to us. He is proud of us. We have shown what we can do. We are ready.

My mother goes upstairs to the loft. She cannot account for who I have become; aloof, in long skirts, silent. She does not want to find what she knows is waiting for her. She opens the trunk. She finds the papers. She reads. She is frozen. She has lost me. She has given me everything and I have escaped her.

She calls my friend's mother, in anguish tells her what she has found, asks what it all means.

I dreaded this call, says my friend's mother.

My mother hangs up. She must do this alone. She calls my father, my grandparents, she calls the bishop, she calls the head-mistress. She does not call the police. She does not call me. She gathers forces, gathers herself, preparing to mount a rescue, not knowing I will rescue myself.

We cannot remain at our school. The father has a cottage

waiting for us in France. We learn lies at school and at home
our families tempt us with old ways. It is time for us to live as
God intended. We must find a way to lay our hands on our
passports so that we can travel swiftly with him to France. In
France the law cannot reach him. In France we will be safe and
grow rosemary and learn the subjunctive. We must invent a
school trip so we can ask our mothers for our passports. I feel
the world slipping away. Pink sand through my fingers. I know
I cannot do this. I know I have waded into black water. I know
I cannot see the bottom.

I have no memory of my father in any church. So when he tells
me he is marrying his third wife in a church, and how they have
been meeting with the priest prior to the wedding, and how
much he likes him, I am surprised by this newfound religiosity.
I assume this is the influence of his third wife and I hide my
scorn. A year later the same priest baptizes their daughter, his
third. My father refers to the priest as his friend, invites him
to dinner. This too, I assume, is an offering to his wife. Ten years
later my daughter is born and he sends her a cross with her
initials engraved on it. It is tiny. Small as my thumbnail. He
cannot afford the chain, he apologizes, but he wants her to
have something from her grandfather. I am full of feeling. I am
still surprised. I will supply the chain, I promise him, and I tuck
the little red box in the back of a drawer. After my father dies

I sit on his bed and pick up the book he was reading. It is one I have given him. The page is marked by a small saint's card. It is a little laminated watercolor of Mary in a blue dress, holding a blue flower. They give these out during mass. I am surprised anew that he treasured such things. I leave the card on the nightstand beside his glasses but I bring the book home with me.

I wake alone with my head in my arms, resting on an old etched desk. I have no idea how I got there. I am in my pajamas. My cheeks are wet and the moon spills across the blackboard. I am a ghost haunting my own classroom. I walk a long corridor, climb stairs back to my dorm. I climb back into bed and wait for morning.

My friend reminds me it is time for our daily call to the father. I face the wall. She has an idea for securing our passports. I walk past her. She is puzzled. She tells me I have missed too many calls, it is time, he has pushed us too hard, he knows this, he'd like to talk to me. I head to class. She comes at night, hissing. He has invested so much. I owe him an explanation. Think of what he has spent on us. I roll on my side. I stuff the catechism book in a trash can and dream of hell. We pass each other in silence. I cannot meet her eye. Our friends wonder at our new distance. I have no answers. I have no answers. I sleep and walk and sleepwalk. I go back to chapel and sit at the back saying nothing, singing nothing.

I return from chapel and prepare my books for class. I find a note scrawled in my friend's hand stuffed in my pigeonhole.

"Call my father. Tell him my mother took me."

My friend's mother has arrived unannounced while we were in chapel. She has packed her daughter's things and escorted her silent child to the waiting car. My friend snatched a moment to scrawl this note and leave it for me.

I do not call the father.

Later, much later, we hear that she arrives home, refuses to speak, and goes straight to her room. She will not leave her room. Days later she emerges, asks to play tennis. Her mother is delighted. They play. My friend has a blister, she says, she must go inside for a Band-Aid. Her mother waits on the tennis court. And waits. My friend walks through the house, down the driveway, and into her father's waiting car. Her passport is in her pocket. She spends the next five years in France with him. She never lives with her mother again.

I have not seen her since that day she left school.

This is not the story of my life. This is a story of my life. My mother still trembles at it. She says it was sexual, the interest the father had. I feel heat in my cheeks. I say I never felt that, not once. My father, years later, asks me what it was about. I look away. It feels hardest of all to explain to him what I barely understand myself.

"There was a vacancy," I say. "He filled it."

Gap

I AM EIGHTEEN. I sit in a room with no heating, in a college founded by a libidinous king and his unruly cardinal, and convince three men that I cannot come to Oxford quite yet, that I must have a year to myself first, so I may learn my father before I learn any more. They nod and agree. I have no idea what I am asking for. I ask for a year because it is not always awarded, and I like a challenge. And because my mother thinks it will be good for me. All I have done is study and read for months. I am covered in a rash brought on by the stress, which webs across my stomach, down my legs, and buries itself in my elbows, my knees, my scalp. I sleep in gloves so I cannot scratch myself at night. School ends. It is over. I smoke relentlessly, learn to love the taste of vodka. I am sharp-tongued and soft to kiss and the boys like me. My friends pack rucksacks and vanish in little clusters to India, America, Europe. I buy a ticket to Argentina, alone.

My mother drives me to the airport. I watch the city and the meadows and the flat sky. I wipe my eyes. I do not want to go. I am clenched like a hawk's bill on a snake. My mother reminds me that I never want to go anywhere. I shake my head. I do not want this part of my life to begin.

"It will be good. He has so much to tell you."

I breathe on the window.

"Like when he went to jail?"

My mother looks at me, eyes wide.

"How did you know?"

I shrug.

"I always knew."

Fireworks explode silently beneath my plane as it breaks the clouds, pink and gold chrysanthemums noiselessly blooming through the haze. I have never seen fireworks from above before. But I do not want to see them. I close the shade, lean my head on the window, and pull out a book. Don't look up until you get there.

I live with my grandparents in their smoke-filled flat in Buenos Aires. I live with them because my father lives in a one-bedroom on the outskirts of town, far from the few people I know. I come to spend time with my father but he is working and I am eighteen and what are we supposed to do together, day after day? No one has thought this through. I do not know what is expected of me here. What I know is that I am supposed to be on a grand adventure. I am supposed to be living on trains, loose change, cheap beer, and hard cheese. I am supposed to be having sex with strangers in campsites.

Instead I sleep deep into the hot mornings on the pullout

bed in my grandparents' living room. I wake, roll over, light a cigarette, and listen to my father's father putter in the kitchen. My grandmother reads the newspaper in bed, waits for her breakfast on a tray. He has brought it to her for fifty years. She is brilliant, still a practicing lawyer. She cannot cook. She does not hug. She wears silk shirts and is never more than a wrist flick away from her cigarettes and the tiny brass ashtrays that stud their apartment. I lie and listen to their quiet two-step and wait for my life to begin.

They live in the old embassy quarter of the city, a quiet leafy apartment among the little palaces with their walled courtyards and armed guards, jacaranda trees, and bright flags limp in the sunlight. Opposite, a new mall, American in build, lofty and dazzlingly clean. Everywhere there are cafés. Men sit at metal tables, pastel sweaters tossed over their shoulders, moccasins dangling from tanned bare ankles, sipping at tiny cups, one eye on every woman who enters. Kiosks dot every corner, jeweled with cigarettes, chewing gum, *alfajores*, magazines. The city smells of cigarettes and exhaust smoke and aftershave. Sex lives on the street, double takes from scaffolded buildings, lazy wolf whistles from open car windows, approving clucks from the chorizo vendor's cart. Sex is everywhere and there is none for me. I am drenched with longing. I want to be anywhere but here, in this apartment, listening to my grandfather's devotion and the hum of an air conditioner. I wait for a man to rescue me, my father, a boyfriend, a friend, anyone who will redeem the featureless monotony of these days. My cousin lives with my grandparents too. He works in an office and arrives home late. He rubs his handsome face. He tells me stories of when my mother lived in the city, how much he loved her, how she played with him. It makes me miss her. She feels worlds away. One night, drunk, I pull out the map of the London Underground to show him where we live. We fall out of our chairs laughing at his pronunciation of Leicester, Waltham-stow, Greenwich. He swears he will live in Piccadilly Circus one day. I am drunk with homesickness.

I call my friends here, the family I have known since birth, who live in rambling houses and are always at each other's birthdays, who pause their endless flow to fold me to their hearts every time I visit. This the family that retrieves me from airports and nightclubs and bus stops. This is the kind of family I long for. There are six children. The mother is my mother's best friend. They met through my father and loved each other immediately. The eldest daughter is my best friend. We met each other in our prams. Now we meet daily, make rubbery plans. We drift from house to house, wander into museums, wait for her brother and his friends to decide what they are doing, then squeeze into cars with them, at the mercy of their whims, following them to tiny bars, pizza joints, pool tables. We hover at the edges, waiting to be noticed. All this waiting is unendurable but where else am I to go?

I am bilingual but not completely. The argot is swift, the

cursing elaborate, and I learn it all, slinging invective that is entirely about our mothers' body parts. I long for autonomy. I long for the freedom to travel alone. I spend eight months wishing I were a man. No one here wants to backpack. No one here wants to wear filthy jeans and share beer and a pill and hike over pointless mountains. The girls stretch their limbs into tight white jeans and flatten their hair and their stomachs and wait for their telephones to ring.

My father drops by my grandparents' apartment one evening and we all settle in the living room with its matching pale blue armchairs, silver frames hovering on low glass tables. My grandmother, doting, delighted, offers him the best seat, tells him he looks tired. He asks me to pour him a whiskey and stretches out, elegant, white shirt unbuttoned, loving and remote as only he can be. Beside him his mobile phone sits like a gun wedged between his hip and the armchair. It is new, thick, and improbable. We sit and talk, and I am grateful for the buffer of my grandmother, and it occurs to me that he is too. He squeezes my hand as he tells us about his day, his hand streaked with scars. We are going for dinner, he and I. We have spoken during the day and confirmed it. I have waited all day for him. He seems restless, distracted. I get up to get my bag. As I rise, he picks up his cell phone, as though it had rung, and answers it. I watch him speak into a dead phone. The catamaran teeters on its edge. I watch him animate his face, his hands, gesticulate to me as though he can't believe his ears, shake his head, and talk to no one. I wait for the pantomime to end. I look at my grandmother. She looks away. I look at him. He hangs up. I wait for someone to say something. My father finishes his whiskey and grabs his jacket.

"So sorry, my love. Something came up. Call you in the morning."

He kisses me, reholstering his cell phone, and leaves. I say nothing because I do not yet know what confrontation tastes like. I only know how to swallow salt and look the other way. The elevator sweeps him away from me. I have failed. I have not said the thing I came for. I come back into the living room. I am shaking. My grandmother does not notice or pretends not to. She offers to teach me her card game. I have nowhere else to go. So we play together, smoking, quiet, deep into the night.

A week later I meet my father in a restaurant. The waiter escorts me to his table but a woman is seated there. I look around. She introduces herself. She is my father's girlfriend. She is nervous, smiling, long-faced and short-haired. Her head is small, the hair is cropped close like a boy's, except that even the boys have long hair in this country. I don't know anyone with hair this short. Her eyes are huge and as bright blue as the country's flag. She tells me she's been with my father for a few months, offers me one of her cigarettes. It looks like a lollipop stick. She asks me if I come often to visit him, and how long I plan to stay. She tells me how much my father loves me. We wait for my father to arrive. When he does, he slides in, apologetic, kisses her on the mouth, me on the cheek. She puts her arm around him and keeps it there for the entire meal. She eats nothing. He pets her, pats me. She goes to the restroom and he tells me, wearily, that she is a good person, that she comes from the docks, that her family is rough but that she is a good person. I nod. She walks back toward us. Every man glances up at her as she passes. She is six years older than I am.

Later that summer I go to my father's apartment for dinner. Dinner will be pizza, beer, vodka if he has it. I take a taxi through the city, along the sullen snake-brown river to the suburbs. I let myself into his apartment. He has given me my own key knowing I will never come unannounced. A beer glass filled with splayed-out tulips sits on a smeary table. The room is hot and silent. I slide the doors out to the balcony, inhale as the hot wet flannel of the city slaps my lungs and the city screams far down below. I feel my jeans wrap closer to my body. I wish I'd worn a dress, shorts, anything cooler. I had wanted to look nice for him. It is Friday, the night the city waits for all week, the night I dread. At this hour the nightclubs yawn, awaiting the onslaught, vacant as bouncers. They are vast, open-air, sleek like spaceships. Or they are tiny, cramped, tucked beneath railroad arches. They do not open until midnight but no one is foolish enough to arrive before two. A boy who may or may not be your boyfriend comes to pick you up and take you to the nightclub at around one in the morning. If you cannot conjure a boy to take you then it is permissible to go with a small group of girls. The uniform is strict and unvarying. Jeans you cannot breathe in, platform heels, and tight tops. Long shiny hair that sways and has never known humidity, and little makeup. I cannot find a pair of jeans to fit me in the entire city. I have given up trying. I want to be sipping canned soup on a glacier. I do not want to be drinking bitter espressos at midnight so that a boy who does not love me can pick me up in his father's car and later try to bury his face in my chest. My friends are going out tonight. I feel relieved not to have to go, not to lip-read Spanish passes from sweaty boys with seventies hair and lips like girls, not to feel overweight and overwhelmed in the dark. When they ask me why I cannot come, I shrug, regretful, and say "Papa," and they nod, understanding.

And yet here I am sweating in jeans waiting for a man.

I hear a tap at the balcony door. The girlfriend stands in the doorway. She gestures me inside with her head, her eyes wide and electricity blue. I come in. She has turned on the air-conditioning and the clatter is louder than the city outside. She goes to the kitchen to fix us drinks. Her bottom is high like a soccer ball. A tattoo flashes in the arch of her spine and disappears beneath the waistband as she reaches for tumblers. Without looking at me she tells me my father will be home soon. Home. Because she lives here now. Now I notice the pile of celebrity gossip magazines by the sofa. The scuffed ashtray and smears on the glass tabletop. My father is impeccable in his cleanliness. Fanatical about hygiene, both personal and domestic. His showers are legendary. She hands me a vase of vodka and tonic and tilts her head to one side.

"You have your father's mouth," she says.

I drink before she can kiss me. She knocks hers back, carelessly, and lights her lollipop stick.

"You look so hot in that sweater. Poor baby, you don't know about the summers here, do you?"

I want to tell her how many summers I have spent here, waiting for my father to notice me, but I do not because I realize I don't know if they are that many, or if they were spent here, or in Peru, or in Spain, or in London. But I feel the rising heat at being identified as the outsider. She sashays into the bedroom and I glimpse clothes flung across his neat bed, towels strewn on the floor of the darkened room. She disappears into his closet and emerges with a shimmery slip of gold. It ripples, bias-cut, a honey-colored handkerchief with slender straps. She throws it at me.

"Wear this."

I take it, hating her, and head into the bathroom. It is a windowless oven in here. I ignore my reflection, yank my black cardigan over my head and thrust my way into this slip. It pulls and stretches over my breasts, flares up above my waistband, frilling tightly where it should merely sway. I tug it down. I see black fuzz from the cardigan curled in my armpits and I rinse them out with a washcloth, leaving tiny black worms nestled in the white towel. I fold it and place it carefully back on her side of the sink. Contact-lens solution, a small makeup bag, a neon-pink toothbrush. I look like a girl who borrowed a top that is too small. But it is so hot in here I cannot bear to pull the black cardigan back on. I cannot bear to come out and yet I cannot stay in here either.

I come out. She is smoking a joint. She exhales, offers it to me.

"Your father loves that top."

I take my drink and drain it.

My father arrives later and if he notices the top he does not comment. The girlfriend rolls more joints and orders pizza and I drink vodka and shake my head when the pot is offered to me. We eat pizza and roll out to the balcony to look at the city harsh and loud deep into the night. He tells stories of his days racing Formula One and Formula Three, of polo games and people I've heard of and who have never heard of me. I am buzzed, bored, wondering how I will get back to my grandparents. She listens, eyes blue and blurry with attention. I wonder if she will last long enough to become bored of these stories. He turns on the radio, plays music, and they dance. He keeps her close but not as close as she wants. He looks at me over her shoulder. She nuzzles his neck, whispers in his ear, then peels herself into the bathroom. Alone, he asks me how my day was. I tell him about a modern art exhibit that I've been meaning to go to but haven't actually yet. I tell him I spent the morning there on my own. I describe the friendly gay man who showed me around and the ceramic mobiles that spun in the morning light. I tell him all this so he will not see how utterly at a loss I am, so he will not worry, so he will marvel at his cultured daughter. But he does not see these things because he has never had to see them. He has never had to worry about me because I have never asked him to. He squeezes my knee.

"I'm so glad you're here."

The girlfriend comes out from the bathroom. She is glittery, eyes like the ocean seen through portholes. Now he disappears into the bathroom and she goes to the radio, finds the music my friends are dancing to under the railway arches downtown, turns it up, and dances. She moves like a snake shedding its skin, like the city is watching. I cannot dance like this. My father stands in the doorway watching her. He raises his eyebrows at me. My face aches from smiling. I have somehow found myself in a club. She reaches her slender arms to me, to my father, to join her show. He reaches her, bobbing to the music but continues on to the kitchen to make us more drinks. I swallow a yawn, wondering when I can order my cab.

"He's so happy. Because you're here. Why don't you stay here? She should stay the night!" she calls into the kitchen.

My father leans into the fridge.

"She can stay on the sofa!"

The girlfriend is girlish, pleading. I have stayed here before you, I want to tell her. I will stay here after you. I have been bought by others, by your predecessors, with dolls and dresses and drinks and cigarettes. I know I am not what is of value. I am simply the means by which you may show your devotion. I am the altar, not the god.

My father looks at me.

"You're tired. You should stay here."

He picks up the radio and carries it into the bedroom. The girlfriend wails in protest at the party being over so soon.

"I know her. She's tired and she'll never tell us. So we move in here."

I am grateful and embarrassed. They sweep into the bedroom where the door briefly closes and voices rise and then fall. The door opens and she comes to the couch smiling brightly. She hands me a sheet and starts sweeping away throw cushions. As I get up to help her I see white powder glitter in the cave of her nostril. My father hands me an old T-shirt of his. He kisses me good night. She air-kisses at me as she crosses to their bedroom, balancing the vodka, the ashtray, and an ice bucket. The bedroom door closes. I look down at her golden top, stretched tight, stained, no trace of her body in it. I pull it over my head and pull on his soft worn white one. It smells of laundry powder. I lie down and shiver beneath the thin sheet, finally cold. I wonder what they will do, both high and locked in a small bedroom. I am too tired to care. The music is muffled, is raised and swiftly lowered. I feel it throbbing through the thin walls.

I wake with the yellow light of dawn. My throat is coated, my eyes gummed. I stagger to the bathroom, to find the girlfriend, all legs, leaning into the mirror. She turns to me, surprised, pressing her hands to her face and I see she looks different, younger, stripped. She looks banal. Her eyes are brown like dirt. She looks at me, pleading.

"Don't tell your father. He doesn't know."

She turns back to the mirror and presses a tiny bright blue disk onto her iris.

I fold my sheet, lay it on the sofa, stuff the camisole in the laundry basket. I take the subway home. The city is silent, subdued after the night's excesses. I let myself into my grandmother's apartment, pull out my foldout bed, and curl back to sleep.

My grandmother finds me a companion to travel with. He is the son of a law colleague of hers. She delivers him like a bone in my lap. He and his father come to dinner. He is skinny and pale. He sips wine and nods whenever his father speaks. He is, however, willing to travel with me down to Patagonia. We leave a week later. He procures me a backpack that is really a canvas cage with straps. It is like carrying a camp bed on my spine but I do not care because I am at last doing something, going somewhere. He is entirely wrong for this trip. He belongs at a chamber music group, not a bus stop, but I do not care because at last I am moving, I am leaving the city, I am doing what young people are supposed to do. We take the bus south.

He is eager. A puppy. He has brought poetry to read to me on the interminable bus journey. He has facts to share about where we are going. He has a Walkman full of classical music he thinks I will like. Everything is wrong. We arrive and stretch and walk and find a campsite. I offer to help put up the tent, but he waves me off me, reveling in his spindly chivalry. I try to light a fire to avoid watching him wrestle with the tent. The tent is up. He pulls out his bedroll, hesitates.

"Shall I sleep out here?" he asks.

I tell him that there is no need, we can share the tent, I won't try anything I promise. He looks crushed. I go in search of water and befriend a group of Australians and feel at home for the first time in months. I laugh and split a beer with them. Adopt me, I want to cry. Let me travel with you for the rest of my life. My eyes shine. My companion comes to find me, angry at my defection. I wave him over, he is invited to join, but he sulks on the periphery of the campfire, declines beer, and retires early to our tent. I slink in, late, smelling of beer. He is huddled in a corner. I try to zip the tent and fail. He rolls over and does it for me. It is the last night he sleeps in the tent. I have humiliated him and from this night forward he sleeps outside the tent, parading his self-imposed exile.

He sulks for the entire journey. He walks eight steps behind me up every hill, defers with exaggerated courtesy to my every wish, as though he were a courtier appointed to a visiting dignitary. I am unsure how to react. I wonder if my grandmother is paying him. I wonder what she, or my father, promised him. It dawns on me that what he wants is the clarity of a job description, say, my boyfriend, but this position is not available to him. In the absence of any such category (he disdains to be my friend), he has deemed himself my servant. We hike mountains and lakes and the backpack grinds into my back and I dare not mention it for fear of wounding him further. None of this is as fun as I had thought. It is not fun to gather kindling by a lake with a moody attendant, less fun still to pitch a tent with a silent martyr and sit beneath the stars with a spurned lover who stares moonily into the flames and scrapes his untouched plate into the undergrowth. This, I think, is not how this is supposed to go. We come home after a week. We ride in silence the fifteen hours back to the city. He grimly passes me biscuits, water. I hand back the backpack and he shakes my hand gravely in farewell. I wonder if I should tip him.

I am back in the city, grateful now for its familiarity. My days slip into a rhythm. My father and I glimpse each other when we can, skirting his girlfriend and even the mention of her. I spend weekends at the estancia of my family friends. I watch polo and pretend to care. Friends from England arrive, with real backpacks, tea-stained guide books, and an invitation to join them as they cross into Chile. I take *In Patagonia*, Bruce Chatwin's travel memoir, and we use this as our compass. We hitch rides in trucks, sleep under tarps, in garages, orchards. We wake one morning to find our host has left a dirty bucket

of warm plums outside our tent. A card reads "help yourself."
We feast like piglets, squealing. We rinse our faces in lakes. We
play cards. We are always hungry. We wait with thumbs out,
arms aching by damp roadsides. We press our faces in the window of a Welsh tearoom (old settlers from a century back),
pool our money and sit in brocade chairs with antimacassars,
feast on dark dense fruitcake and white scones and hot Welsh
tea. The owner speaks Spanish with a Gaelic lilt and refills our
teapot many times. He has never left this village. He feels both
foreign and familiar. We leave, legs dangling off the back of a
logging truck slowly arching its way across the foothills and
up into the backbone of the Andes.

We snake up through Chile. We live on pisco sours, chips,
and ceviche. Our tongues pucker from all the lemon juice. We
camp at the base of a green volcano and on a stony island of
wild horses. We swim in hot springs. We play more cards. We
reach Santiago and it is time for me to return. The group is
disbanding, splintering into Peru, Venezuela. I take the bus
back to Buenos Aires. I am filthy, I am calloused, I am happy.

It is my mother's birthday. I will surprise her by returning
home. It is as good a reason as any, it has been six months and
I can think of no other way to politely leave. My father suggests
we go away together for a long weekend before I return to
England. It is the only time that we do this. He borrows a
friend's apartment by the beach and we drive down together.
We chatter in Spanish, he marvels at my fluency and I inwardly

preen, outwardly brush it off. We eat fried fish and walk the windswept beaches. We share cigarettes and tell stories about the past. I speak of Oxford and wonder what it will be like. He tells me he cannot wait to visit, see it for himself (he never comes). He steps away to answer his phone. His wallet lies limp on the table. I pick it up, leaf through it. I find what I know I will find, a wrap of cocaine carefully folded among the few notes. I dab my thumb and rub it on my gums. It tingles and I wrap it up, tuck it back. I wonder how the weekend will unfold if I tell him I have tried it too. I wonder why he needs cocaine to spend one weekend with his daughter. And just how much jail time he needs to do before he will stop taking it. I wonder how he can afford it.

We drive back to the city locked in hot chaotic traffic. Cars steam and jolt beside us. We listen to music. My father, without looking at me, asks me not to mention to his girlfriend that he has spent the weekend with me.

"She thinks it was a work thing," he says.

I stare ahead. I can taste blood. I will not swallow it now.

I tell him I will not lie for him. I tell him I am not his mistress, I am his daughter. He should spend the weekend with me. He should have spent all the weekends with me. She is not his equal. She is a child. No one in the family can stand her. Nothing about her is good enough. He looks at me now, surprised. We are neither of us used to the sound of my voice. He nods.

"You are right," he says, and squeezes my knee.

I fly home a few weeks later. My mother is confused, delighted, scrambles to make sense of my presence after so long away. I am the exact age she was when she married him. I am blond and bilingual. I know everything there is to know and I am a child. I am ready for my life to begin.

He splits up with the girlfriend a month after I leave.

Need

I AM SITTING in a cold bath in an attic in northern Ireland, weeping. I am twenty-two. My grandmother is dead. My mother's mother is gone. She of the sweet peas and the tennis court and the soft hair and the skirted swimsuits. She who brings herself breakfast in bed, leaves the milk in a glass jar on the windowsill, and eats bran flakes while listening to the World Service. She who taught me tennis and grace and how to cut a rose. I am stunned. My grandfather died only two weeks earlier. His was a long death. We are quietly relieved that the waiting is over and we bring my grandmother to our home to stay with us. She sits at the dining-room table, writing letter after letter in her exquisite looped handwriting, acknowledging every word of condolence she is offered after fifty years of a difficult marriage. She is tired, deeply tired. She sleeps soundly, has trouble with her pearls in the morning. I go to Ireland for a party. I kiss her goodbye carelessly, innocently.

My host's mother wakes me with the news. She sits at the end of my bed. I am still drunk, still in costume, black kohl streaked across my eyelids. She lays her hand on my foot.

I am dazed. She has it wrong, I think. She means my grand-father. He died. We buried him. She shakes her head. My mother called. She will arrange my flight. She is so sorry, so very very sorry. I lock myself in the bathroom until it is time for me to leave. My hangover is indecorous. I am ashamed of myself. I do not want the party to be over. I do not want my grandmother to be dead. I want to go home.

My grandmother dies in a London street. She decides to see a movie with a friend, her first excursion since the funeral. They leave the cinema, discuss tea, but my grandmother is tired, wants to go home. Ferocious in her frugality as well as her independence, she refuses a taxi and insists on taking a bus. She dies of a heart attack, a broken heart, stepping off the bus, a woman in a silk scarf with an empty purse, a sliver of a wed-ding band, and a bus ticket in her palm. The police have no idea who she is and no way of identifying her. It grows late, the city darkens. My mother calls the friend, who confirms the bus journey but has no more to offer. My mother drives around the city, peering down alleyways, stopping to call home, think-ing any moment she will walk in the front door. No, my step-father says, she is not here. No, my brother says, she has not come. She calls the local police station. She calls another. Gen-tly, they ask her to come in. My mother sees the corner of my grandmother's scarf on a metal table and crumples.

My mother cannot stop crying. She is consumed with shock, with guilt, with funeral arrangements. I need my father. I call

him. I do not know what else to do. I ask him to come. I tell
him I need him. I have never said this to him before. He arrives
two days later. He holds my mother tight and keeps my hand
in his from the moment he arrives. He seems both bewildered
and entirely at home. He has not returned to Europe since he
left jail. He sleeps in my brother's bedroom. He has nowhere
else to stay in this city he once called home. My stepfather
pours them both whiskeys, makes jokes about how much
money my father owes him. We all laugh nervously. My father
offers to pay for my brother's school fees, since my stepfather
has paid for mine. The catamaran dips on its side. We smile
and change the subject.

The church is hot with lilies and people. My grandmother
is deeply loved. No one is ready to say goodbye to her. I read a
poem. It is about triumph and disaster and meeting those two
imposters just the same. It is the epigraph above the entrance
to the center court of Wimbledon, a place where my grandmother triumphed in her youth. My father has never heard
me read, perform, speak anything out loud. He never sees a
single play of mine. I read it for him as well as for her. He nods,
proud, approving, squeezes my knee. He moves among the
family, shy and touched by how many faces light up on seeing
him. He has not felt beloved for a long time, not on any shore.

After the funeral there is a wake and after the wake, we
gather at home. My aunts, raucous and red-eyed, sing and
drink, and my father moves in our midst, no longer shy, no

longer a satellite nor a distant star but a planet in our solar system. They start stories and splinter into new ones. They remember the dead, the living, the forgotten. Through the cigarette smoke, through the grief, they see each other thirty years ago. They nod and remember and laugh and they are twenty-five again, newly hatched. We sing till our throats are hoarse, we smoke and weep and it seems the night will never end. My brother's arms are around my father, my stepfather and I embrace, my aunts entangle with my mother, all the pairings form and reform. I feel unraveled and whole. We are mourning and elated. This is what my grandmother does, she is the place where everyone comes together.

In the morning I drive to show him around the university from which I have already graduated. We walk the damp cobbled streets in the drizzle. We dizzy the spires. I show him the meadow, the cathedral, the libraries. I seem always to be giving my father a guided tour of my life. I miss belonging. I am already a tourist here. He buys a sweatshirt with the city's name on it. We hug fiercely at the airport. I thank him for coming. I tell him I could not have got through it without him. His eyes fill. He wears the sweatshirt on the flight home.

Siblings

MY CHILDREN ARE COMPETITIVE to a degree that is ferocious and absurd. They compete for their father's love as though it were a finite commodity, as though he never gave it to them, as though he only lived with us from time to time, instead of working from home in his upstairs office, ministering to every blister and errant Lego block. They live in the unfiltered sunlight of his love every single day. I marvel at how unstintingly they are loved. But more I marvel at what it is to know yourself with another human by your side, to sift your experience through two people. My husband and I bicker about why there are no avocados in the house. I watch the children raise eyebrows at each other, smile into their oatmeal. I think about all that those raised eyebrows contain. All the reassurance of a face that feels what you are feeling and says, Yes, me too, this is strange, but I am here and you are here and if we are both here, feeling this strangeness, then life is less frightening, more bearable. Then I watch them claw each other over whose turn it is with the ball or the book and I ask my husband, who grew up with a sister, "Is this too much fighting? Or is this the right amount of fighting?"

In my experience fighting is rupture. It is a kind of madness to be the only child of divorced parents who live continents apart. It is schizophrenic. There is no one to hold the pieces with you in their hands, to say, Yes, this is strange, love is different in these houses, and we must be different in these different houses. At each meeting we must uncouple not only from the parent we left behind but from ourselves. Each splintering happens in silence and alone.

And yet I am not alone. I am an only child with three siblings. All four of us are only children. I do not know I am lonely until I am older. I only know my hot attic at my mother's house, painted red, with the dollhouse and the homework I assign my dolls and then sit and complete myself otherwise how will it get done, the skylight window under which I drag the mattress and crack the window and listen to the planes flying over London and floodlit football in the park. In this room, I can be Heidi in Grandfather's hayloft, or Lucy in the wardrobe, or Caroline, my imaginary friend who is very pretty and slightly better at everything than I am. Only the heads of the adults fit through the entrance to the loft. Disembodied they haul themselves up the red ladder to check on me or make me come down. This is what I know. Or I know my father's house, which is wherever he is. It is not until I am older, at school, that I see what it is to have a sibling, to know what music to listen to, to have someone to borrow things from, be exasperated by, to share with and carve yourself in opposition to. There might have been a brother or a sister on that mattress beside me beneath a London sky. There might have been someone to whisper to at night and wonder where our father was, or when we might see him again.

My mother and stepfather have a son who is born when I am thirteen. I love this baby with my soul. He is fat, contented, a prince. He unites us like a new flag. But he arrives just as I depart. I am at boarding school the night he is born. I have already left home. We never live together, we only share the same house. He does not have my father. We barely share a mother, so different are her circumstances now, married, older, solvent, sheltered, secure. He is my brother and I will hold my hand in fire for him. And I am an only child.

My father leaves jail with his wallet and a watch. My stepmother divorces him while he is serving his time. She never lays eyes on him again. She stipulates that my adopted sister no longer carry his last name and she changes it to her own. He has pawned her jewelry, spent her money, slept with her friends, and lied to her face. He has nothing left of value for her to take so she takes his daughter. He has no resources with which to appeal and nothing to offer. He is furious and unmanned.

To this day, my stepmother stays in touch with me and my mother. Birthday cards, Christmas wishes, arrive reliably from

Peru. Nothing elaborate. A thread slung around the earth that we may tug on. But my adopted sister slides out of my life in much the same way she slides into it. She evaporates.

I am at Oxford. I receive a letter. My stepmother and adopted sister are coming to London, would like to take me to lunch. I have not seen them for ten years. I take the bus down from Oxford and we meet in an elegant restaurant in Chelsea. My stepmother looks the same, husky and fragile. She has remarried, the very lawyer who divorced her and my father, but we do not speak of that. My adopted sister smiles shyly, rolls bread crumbs into pellets on the stiff white tablecloth. We speak of safe subjects, of the university, my mother, holidays, the recent cease-fire with the terrorists in Peru. We do not speak of my father. We pick delicately at our salads and the past. As coffee is brought and dessert waved away, my stepmother comes to the point. My adopted sister is getting married. Since it is "impossible" for my father to attend, she would, they would, like to invite me to represent his side of the family and be a signatory at the wedding. I look at the girl beside me who has barely spoken. I offer my congratulations. She is the first person I know who is getting married. It seems indecent. She blushes and looks down.

"We are here to buy her trousseau," my stepmother says.

I fly to Lima. I stay with my former stepmother and her new husband. It is the first society event in years. The city has been paralyzed by terrorist attacks, curfews, and lockdowns. I walk the high-walled garden, watch it transform into a white silk hot-air balloon as men in blue uniforms drape a vast tent around every tree, enfolding, enclosing the night sky, threading branches with invisibly tiny lights. Orchids drip from tree trunks. Everything is illuminated. A man wraps every tree trunk in silk, like the fetlocks of a racehorse. The mist hangs like more silk.

The night before the wedding, my adopted sister and I share a room. We have not shared a postcard for ten years and now here we are, side by side in a double bed, staring at the ceiling. Outside, men on ladders urgently wrap the slender birches. She asks me about our father. I tell her he is a loving man who does not know how to be a father. I tell her I think of him more as a godfather, that she should do the same. I tell her he misses her. I tell her he wishes he could be there. I tell her he is so sorry for all the pain he has caused her. I lull her to sleep with lies so she will glide into her new life feeling the myth of a father's love at her back. The white silk billows and shifts in the soft night air. We listen to it rustle as we once listened to the jungle. She is calm. She is inscrutable. She is eighteen. She is a lagoon with tiny pearls on its dark floor waiting to be found.

I have not told my father I am going to this wedding. He is angry with my stepmother, at how the divorce was handled, at the severity of his exile. He is ashamed of himself but he will never ever say this. Until the day he dies there is a photo of his adopted daughter on his desk, frozen behind glass, in a smocked pink dress and a steady smile. He rarely speaks of her.

I decide to tell him that I am going to the wedding only once I am back from it.

The wedding is Catholic, impenetrable, mystical. Full of incense and bleeding statues. I sign my name in a book and take photos with the family. I am at once the inner circle and the least qualified person to be there. I know no one other than the bride, my stepmother, and her two other children, grown now, who are loving, welcoming, no longer brooding adolescents adrift in an alien city. They are protective of their mother and sister but they know I come in peace. No one mentions my father's name. My adopted sister's face is as frozen and immaculate as a wedding cake. I do not remember her husband. They divorce three years later.

We gather inside the hot-air-balloon garden, the floodlit pepper trees, the dance floor suspended over the swimming pool. Ladies with tight faces and stiff men in white waistcoats approach me, smile, and drift away. No one knows what to do with me but everyone is flawlessly polite. A bachelor is assigned to make conversation with me. He is urbane, well traveled, impeccable. He takes me to brunch the next morning, picks me up in a silver convertible, hands me a silk scarf for my hair, and drives me to a hilltop restaurant far outside the city. I feel like Grace Kelly. I wonder if he plans to murder me or to propose. We walk around the terrace to sit above a cloud bank. He assures me it is the greatest view in Lima and orders us fiery Bloody Marys and a platter of seafood. The sun grows hotter.

He orders more drinks. He lights my cigarette and asks me the questions he actually came for. Where is of my father? What happened to him? Where does my adopted sister really come from? Is she truly adopted or is it a story concocted to conceal an indiscretion of my stepmother's? Or even of my father's? Below us the ocean emerges like a stained blue tablecloth. The sun dazzles hopelessly. The fog has settled damp and heavy inside me. I am dizzy with vodka and the bright light and the strain of smiling for three days straight, but I assure him primly of my sister's origins. I tell him my father is a brilliant man. I tell him we have nothing to hide. I ask him to take me home.

I return to London and call my father, reasoning he may, after all, be proud of me for going in his place, grateful that he was represented at all at his daughter's wedding. He is not grateful, he is disbelieving, then hoary with disdain. I taste my father's rage for the first time. He is vicious, he accuses me of deceit, treachery, gross betrayal. He is disgusted by me. He hangs up.

I sit on my mother's bed holding the phone. I am blank, drained, a bloodless vein. My mother is listening (does she know, does she know it will end this way, she must know or why would she be there). She holds my hand. The shock abates. The blood returns. I am a pulsing artery now. I am outraged. My father has been untouchable my entire life. I have swallowed reproach, eaten regret, defended him from all attacks, shorn myself of pain so that he may continue to bask in my love, so that he will not disappear completely from me. And now he has pushed me off his knee, scorned and disapproved of me. My mother listens, hands me the phone.

"Call him back."

(My mother is nineteen. She asks him where he has been. He tells her not to nag. She pleads. He storms out of the house, slams the front door. She waits. For days she waits. One night he slides between the sheets, lays his hand on her thigh. He does not explain. He does not apologize. She learns never to ask him anything.)

I call him back. It is one of the only fights we ever have, my father and I. I tell him I refuse to be hung up on. It is one more way he has of disappearing. He has disappeared on one daughter, he does not get to disappear on me. I tell him I still have a sister even if he has given up on having a daughter. I tell him I take my responsibilities seriously, even if he does not. I tell him I will guard what he is incapable of protecting. I am pious, anointed with the sanctimony of youth. He is angry, then silent. He does not apologize to me, nor I to him. We recover, because neither of us can afford to lose the other.

I am twenty-seven. I am in my apartment with the fruit rats and the avocado tree. I am folding laundry. My father calls me. He asks what I am doing, what I am reading, how my last audition went. We speak often these days. He clears his throat.

"I want to say sorry."

I ask him what for.

"For all that I missed."

His voice thickens. He tells me his third daughter just took her first steps. He tells me that he was not there for mine, that he was not there for so many of my firsts. He asks my forgiveness for all that he did not see. I sit on the bed holding a damp towel. I tell him it is okay, I don't remember them either, that we have this, we have now, which is more than most people have. He insists and eventually I hear him.

"Thank you," I say. "Thank you."

On my next visit, I watch this new daughter climb into his lap. I sit in his home office, in a patch of sun, smoking, talking. She listens to us, plays with his face, and he listens to me but not with his eyes. She unspools herself from his body and he reaches for her, wanting more. She pushes him away. His hands yearn and she pushes him away. I cannot fathom such carelessness. I have never pushed my father's hands away. I have only ever reached for them.

I am thirty-two. I tell my father it is time he reached out to his adopted daughter in Peru. It has been too long. It is time. He can find her online. He can reach her now without needing permission from her mother. She is a lovely grown woman, remarried, forgiving, with a child of her own, a child who is

the same age as his third daughter. He is a grandfather, I tell
him. They make contact. He is elated. She offers to visit him.
He readily agrees. My adopted sister travels to Buenos Aires,
bringing her daughter with her. They meet for tea in the lobby
of a beautiful old hotel, father and daughter and their two
respective children. (My former stepmother, ever the protector,
accompanies her, but stays upstairs in her suite, does not join
them.) My father calls me, dizzy with relief and joy. He is proud
of himself for coming up with this plan. He is full of news of
his recovered daughter. I realize I am relieved. I had feared
feeling jealous. But I am relieved because the readiness with
which my father turned his back on a child has haunted me
since I was old enough to understand what had happened. We
stay in baggy touch, the reunited siblings and the offspring, a
comment here and there on each other's pages, birthday wishes,
an annual photo. Everyone is loving, circumspect, and relieved.

There is one more daughter.
    Perhaps.
    I have never met her.

I am twenty-seven. I am in my apartment with the fruit rats
and the avocado tree. I am reading a script on my laptop. An
email from my father arrives. The subject line is "Guess who?!"

I open it. It is a forwarded advertisement for an eyeglass company. A young woman in black-rimmed glasses sits at an office desk, smiling at the camera. Below her is an offer for discounted eyeglasses. Below the advertisement my father has written, in bold and all caps: "SHE SAYS SHE IS YOUR SISTER!!!!!"

I read it again. The phrasing makes no sense. It sounds accusatory, as though somehow I have misled this young woman. The exclamation marks suggest something funny, prankish, hilarious. None of which I feel. I pick up the phone.

He tells me the young woman in the photo has been in touch. She claims my father is her father. He tells me he has no idea if this is true. I ask if it is possible. He admits yes, it is possible, that he knew her mother, that yes, they had an affair in Peru, while he was married to my stepmother, but it was brief, he had no idea she was pregnant, he never heard from her again. He tells me he is insisting on a paternity test. I zoom in on the face. She has a face like a heart, toasted skin, dark eyes. She shares his angled cheekbones that look like someone has split bread with a honey knife. I close my eyes, exit the screen. I tell him he cannot hand me another sister like this, via a forwarded online advertisement. That we all deserve actual data and then we will see. My father lives in a borrowed apartment, on borrowed money, with his third wife in a separate bedroom and his third daughter, two years old, clambering over him. There is barely enough of him to go around for those of us who have a legitimate claim to him.

I do not know if a paternity test ever took place. She looks more like him than any of us. Her story is not mine to tell, only where it meets my root system and nudges at it. I see her on the Internet. She makes shrines to him, a man she never knew. She places votive candles and toy racing cars and artificial flowers in front of a photocopy of a photo of him that I own. I find myself unable to look and unable to look away. Is this so different from what I am doing, I wonder. I do not want to share him with her. I do not want to share, like the only child I am. He fathered four only children. I am the eldest of those four. We each live in the shadow of our mothers, sheltered by them, jealously guarded by them, each with a story of our own neglect and love. My story is all I have.

I am a dog with a splinter of a bone growling at an empty street.

Se Cayó

I AM FORTY-TWO. I am on my way to the airport to bury my father. I realize that my adopted sister does not know he is dead. That no one has told her. I have no number for her. I must call my former stepmother. We have not spoken for years. Her voice is the same, deep and earthed. She says my name with love. The freeway whizzes past. I see the gray-white light of Los Angeles, the frizzed-out electric pallor of the airport. I taste the words on my tongue, in Spanish, familiar but new, raw and bloody.

"*Se cayó*," I tell her.

He fell.

He fell.

He fell.

Adrenaline

HE FELL in all the ways there are to fall. Short, out, apart, in love, from grace, afoul of the law, by the wayside, off the map.

The word *accident* has "fall" in its very root. The word is formed from *ad* (toward) and *cadere* (to fall). To fall toward. To befall. It is defined as "anything that happens without forethought or expectation, an unforeseen course of events." This reads like a working definition for my father's life.

It is hard to compete with adrenaline when you are a child. Children are the opposite of adrenaline. They are routine, grinding, and inexorable repetition. Any parent knows this. Adrenaline is the tingling of freedom in the wrists, the immanence of chaos. I am a young child and already I know that my father loves me utterly and yet without precision, that he is vague on the details of my life because he disdains the quotidian, because the focus of his attention is always somewhere just beyond the horizon. My mother loves me steadily as the ocean.

When he is fourteen he steals his father's car, drives it four blocks into a lamppost. It is a write-off. My grandfather grounds him for months, withholds all pocket money, all privileges. My father sneaks out anyway, steals money from his mother's purse, puts the new car in neutral and pushes it up the slope of the under-ground garage so no one will hear the engine. Eighteen months later, he crashes the new car. He pulls himself free of the wreck-age, surveys the damage, trembling, convinced his father will actually kill him this time. The police arrive. My father decides to faint. (He is already an expert at leaving.) He wakes up in the hospital, overhears doctors tell his parents that their son will never walk again. He hears their sobs but knows this is not true. He knows he already walked out of that wrecked car. He knows he has told his body to shut down in order to protect himself from his father's fury. And now he must tell his body to resurrect itself. This is the story he believes. But his body does not cooperate. He is paralyzed from the waist down. He spends months in traction, undergoes months of rehabilitation. He tells himself that he has done this to himself, so he can undo it to himself. He walks out of the hospital six months later.

"Beware the mind," he tells me.

I am five. My father disappears in a biplane over the Amazon. He and the pilot are missing for days, with no trace of the plane. They are presumed dead. He is discovered unconscious, hanging from a tree, his chair dangling from a branch by the seat belt, by the Paraguayan army, which happens to be on exercise in the area. They cut him down, patch him up, return him to England, where he tells the story with relish.

I am one. I have just learned to walk. My parents drive home from my grandmother's house, arguing. My mother holds me in her arms in the front seat. A car careens toward them, on the wrong side of the road, on the motorway. It is a head-on collision, utterly unavoidable. My father's reflexes are so swift that he turns the wheel to take the impact on his side as my mother hurls me into the backseat. Both of my parents fly through the windshield. I tumble into the footwell behind them and am unharmed, although I refuse to walk again for another year. They are sedated and stitched and carry scars on their heads and hands. The driver of the other car is killed outright. We all should have been.

My father decides to take up flying. He has money now, wives, children, mistresses, polo ponies. Now he wants to fly. He drives with his best friend to an airfield outside London. From the air traffic control tower, they survey the countryside. He spots a neighboring racetrack. He points.

"Wait," he says. "That's what I want to do."

My father already drives like a race-car driver. His hands are filmy with scars. The hobby consumes him. He drives competitively. He pays for the cars himself. He drives Formula One and Formula Three. He never wins, never places, but loves the competition, the focus, the speed. The whine of the racetrack is the soundtrack of my weekends with him. My stepmother refuses to attend and watch him risk his life. I watch videos of his races with him, his face close to the screen, hands on his thighs, urging himself on. I play with dolls at his feet.

The prime minister's son wants to race the Paris–Dakar Rally with my father as his copilot. My father refuses, says the man is a clown. The clown races anyway, gets lost in the desert, has to be rescued, makes international headlines. My father laughs. Later he is named in a scandal that involves the clown and an arms deal. He does not laugh now. His name is in the papers. He is summoned to Downing Street. The woman who runs the country scarcely lifts her enormous head as he is ushered in.

"Was my son involved?" she asks, still writing.

My father assures her that neither he nor her son have any involvement, have never heard of the men in question, never even met them, nothing could be further from the truth. She waves him away and continues to write.

He does not race again.

New wife. New hobby. I am twenty-five. My father is fifty-seven. His girlfriend, who will become his third wife and the mother of his third daughter, has eyes full of mirth and a throat she hurls back to the sun when she laughs, which is often. She smells of cigarettes and espresso beans. She knows the best cafés in the city and spends hours charming every waiter with her easygoing smile. Everything about her is relaxed. She is the only woman I know there who does not straighten her hair. She lies in bed eating ice cream out of the carton, air-conditioning blasting, watching hour upon hour of soap operas. She does not have a job. I have never met a woman with so little shame around her indolence. She relaxes in her full body, laughs at my father's pretensions, indulges his endless stories about the past, befriends his friends, and brings my father back to life. She nudges him back into the world.

They spend weekends at an estancia that belongs to an old friend of my father. The friend is a former society girl who, like him, has tasted disgrace, an aristocrat brought low by a very public drug conviction, who must live off her land now. She and her sons retreat to the country and learn to farm.

Society closes its doors to them all, and so she lives here, in the country, dragging her patch of land into fruition, astride a tractor in a faded gold bikini and a cowboy hat. She and my father grew up together, a dazzling pair of reprobates. When he returns from his time in jail, this is the friend who throws her doors open in welcome, in recognition, in relief.

Her home becomes his retreat, a safe place to escape the heat and the hate of the city, and replicate the familiar rhythm of going to the country for the weekend. My grandparents have sold their property to pay for his legal fees, and he is no longer welcome in the estancias he used to go to, so every weekend, he and his new wife drive two hours to the sprawling farm to lie by the pool flecked with green, play backgammon, drink whiskey, and swap old tales of past extravagance.

One weekend he sees men falling from the sky. Bright balloons suspend them. They hang, they fall, they dance above him. He watches them, stick figures, against the vastness of white sky, suspended over the endless horizon of the pampa.

The next day he drives a few miles to the airfield. It comprises a small runway, a hangar, and a bar. Mismatched plastic chairs and tables sit by the runway, dotted with big red plastic ashtrays, stained and sun-bleached. He sits at the bar, orders a beer. His wife pulls up a chair in the sun, tips her head back, stretches her long limbs on the tarmac, lights a cigarette, pulls out a magazine. He watches as men arrive, young men who unload their gear from battered cars, men who wear their brown hair long, working men who clap each other on the back, who greet the other men like brothers, who hand over hard-earned pay after a week of teaching or trucking or motorbike messengering through the swerving city to zip up their suits and pack their chutes and step into their harnesses and pile into an old Cessna with open sides and a bench seat and climb higher and higher above the cloud line, and pull down their goggles and strap on their helmets and step out into the unsolid air. He imagines the open door. He pictures the tumbling white, the roar of the engine, the rigidity of the doorframe, the softly infinite drop before it, the nearness of nothingness, the no place of the threshold. He watches the men reappear through the clouds, billowing, aloft, descending, alive, ignited. He watches the fog of debt, drudgery, duty evaporate from their eyes. He watches them land lighter, purified, baptized by free fall. He remembers that cleansing flame. It has been years since he felt that light.

He watches from the ground, but only once.

To skydive you must first jump in tandem, strapped with your back embedded in an instructor's chest. The instructor orchestrates the entire jump, pulls the rip cord at the correct moment, lets the chute open so it will tug you both up up up by the armpits like the yanked chain of an angry dog, while you then float down slowly, wheeling in wide circles as you make your descent. It is the tourist's jump. You are a sightseer, a voyeur. My father jumps twice in tandem on the first day. His wife watches, sips her beer, befriends the bartender. My father goes back the next day, jumps twice again. All week in the city his feet itch. He cannot wait to go back. He dreams of the fall, of the peace, of the quiet roar above the world.

I am in Los Angeles. I am trying to make a career, friends, money. I do yoga in the mornings, write short stories in the afternoons, and wait for a role that might change my life. My father tells me he has taken up skydiving. Of course you have, I think, of course. Isn't that what I should be doing, I wonder. It is not the first time that I wonder if he is the one really living life while I am always waiting for it to happen to me.

He completes twenty jumps, fifty, a hundred. He spends his entire weekends at the airstrip. He buys rounds of cold beer for the boys, as he calls them, earns first their grudging respect and soon their unswerving devotion. They are twenty, thirty years his junior. Most have never left the country, few the continent. None of them has a leather briefcase in the trunk and a wife sunbathing at a nearby estancia. But despite the differences in age, income, and experience they love him. They call him Lion. He is their mascot, proof that age need not mean numbing conventionality, nor the death of liberty. (His wife soon tires of the plastic chairs, the warm wine, and the airstrip gossip and retreats to the filmy pool back at the house. She plays cards in the shade, smokes tiny joints twisted like firecrackers, and laughs with her friend.)

I visit my father and we often stay here at this house. The friend is carelessly, endlessly hospitable, opening rooms for me, imposing nothing but her generosity on us all. I wander from room to room in this house that is not mine, nor anyone in my family's. I feel like a rube, unsophisticated, out of place. Every night the aging hipsters relive their youth, get high, sway around low coffee tables cluttered with silver photo frames of elegant people in tailored cream pantsuits and low-backed dresses. They wait till I have gone to bed to pull cocaine from their beautiful old wallets and line it up with practiced ease on the card table. In the morning I rise before everyone, walk past silent bedrooms fat with slumber, sit in the ruined living room as the maid quietly gathers glasses, ashtrays, plates. I hover in the kitchen desperate to make my own coffee, forage for my own breakfast. But this is not my house.

I lie in the sun and bake like a pastry until I am too burned to breathe, too swollen to sit. I take ibuprofen between my cracked lips and lie on my bed under the air-conditioning and sweat and cool and sweat again and wonder if it's possible to die of sunburn. It feels like my heart is blistering. My father's friend wanders past, her ropy abdomen taut and bronzed, a white Stetson on her dirty-blond hair, a dangling cigarette and a clinking glass of whiskey. She nods as she passes my open door, raises her glass in salutation.

"Gone again?" she asks.

Yes. My father is skydiving, again. He is licensed now, a

free-faller. He tumbles out of planes like other people pour themselves a drink. He soars, suspended between air and gravity, belly down, feet down, head down, then pulls the rip cord to float to earth.

I take my boyfriends to meet my father. It is a rite of passage for us all. They have heard the stories. I bring a boyfriend who is an actor, bird-boned, pale as a wrist in winter. He is a redhead, delicate, and very very funny. He is as far from my father as it is possible to travel. He comes with me to Argentina. We stay at my father's friend's house, the farm in the countryside near the airstrip. Her sons are visiting. They are polo players, models, they look as though they have wandered in from a nearby photo shoot. My boyfriend with the red hair is riveted. He studies them like alien life. He says it is like glimpsing my father's younger self.

My father is going skydiving. He asks my boyfriend if he would like to jump. We have prepared for this. It is inevitable. He says he will. We rise early for breakfast. We sit in the kitchen, sharing coffee, toast. One of the sons walks in. He is wearing only his underwear. The air tightens. He is golden, sleep-creased, muscled. His underwear gleams stretched and white. He leans lazily across the table, his crotch suspended in our faces as he reaches for the coffeepot. He asks my boyfriend in his broken English if he plans to jump today. My boyfriend says he does. The son stretches and points outside.

"I'm gonna fly," he says.

The son heads outside. He swigs his espresso, straps a para-glider to his naked back, and runs and rises from the lawn like a motorized demigod, escaping over the blue eucalyptus trees into the white sky.

My boyfriend laughs and laughs and laughs. He wonders to what land I have brought him where the most beautiful men in the world strap a lawnmower to their backs and disappear into the void.

Years pass. Three boyfriends of mine jump from planes with my father. I suppose if he owned a boat we would go sailing. But he does not. So we do not. They jump. The farm changes, the crops yield, the sofas are reupholstered, the pool paved, my father's room now has a rug, a television, and a baby in it. This is his third daughter, a moon-faced brown-eyed nugget who folds into my shoulder. She is three months old and asleep in her mother's arms when my father falls like a meteor into the earth.

He is high when he boards the Cessna that morning. He makes a small tight joint and smokes it alone in his car. He stashes his wallet and bag of weed beneath the front seat, gets out, and goes to suit up. He goes up in the plane, makes small talk with the boys, about the week, the weather, someone else's jump. He arrives at twelve thousand feet and steps out, a man descending. He falls, upright at first, wind whipping his face, pummeling his cheeks, his lips, drumming his eardrums. Adrenaline thrums in his neck. With his thumb he can block out his battered car parked in the tiny lot; he can obliterate the estancia that is not his, where his wife and baby sleep in a borrowed bed. He falls so fast and so slowly. Time stops and hurtles toward him. He falls and dips facedown and spins and the great barrel of his chest slices through the atmosphere and he laughs at the extraordinary simplicity of it all and too late he realizes it is time to open. By the time he finishes the thought, the chute is sagging behind him, not billowing, not netting wind resistance in its bright silk and slowing down the force of his descent. By the time he finishes the thought his life is already irrevocably changed. You must complete at least two wide slow turns to take the speed off before landing. He barely completes one and drives into the ground with the force of a man falling from a corn silo. He lifts one leg, his right one, to save what he can, and he takes the full impact in his left. The tibia shatters and the fibula splinters, they rupture the skin.

My father faints instantly from the pain. The men in the hangar race toward him convinced they have watched him die. They run to him, screaming back for help. I am nauseous as I write this. We are in rehearsal for his death. I do not want to imagine the awkward angle of his leg, the earth and his blood commingling. I do not want to imagine my father unconscious in a field with that fluttering silk canopy behind him, the men running toward him, the implacable immensity of that enormous sky. I refuse it, as I refuse his wrecked body on a rooftop fifteen years later.

My father takes his chances with every law, even gravity.

A friend calls me. I am in Los Angeles, working on a show about marriage. I am told he has fallen and landed badly, that he's alive, that he's in a hospital, that he has been badly hurt but it's all his leg, not his head nor his spine. I am told he's lucky, he's a lion, he's a survivor. I am meant to feel relieved. Instead I am confused, I am numb. I wonder at what point in my life I will cease to get shattering phone calls about my father. I wonder if I will ever shock him instead.

I sit by his bed in the hospital. He is white like a skull. There is a vast cage suspending the sheet over his leg like a tent so that nothing can touch his ruined limb, and no one can see it. He is on morphine, a warm weak smile spreads across his face as he wakes. He was not expecting me. His eyes fill. My father never cries. I sit on his bed and hold his hand, I cup his face. I want to cup his face now. I stroke the back of his scarred hands with my thumb. It's okay, you're okay, you're alive, I am here. He's unable to speak. He turns his head into the pillow. He is shame. He is fear. He is relief.

"I'm sorry," he whispers. "I'm sorry."

He is soft, he is pale, he is yellow, he is an unmade bed with glittering eyes. He is alive.

Aftermath

IT TAKES SEVEN YEARS and eighty operations, using bone from his ribs, his femur, and skin from his torso, to try to build my father a new leg. So bad is the break and so deep the infection that nothing holds. The very marrow of his bone is infected, rejects all grafts, all surgeries. Nothing can reach it. My father, who strode the world, dangled from jungles in Paraguay and traded scrap metal in Vietnam, skied the Alps, swung race cars around Brands Hatch, tamed horses and women, cannot pull up his own pants.

His study now becomes his bedroom and his self-appointed clinic. A single cot in one corner, a bedside table covered with bandages, dressings, topical creams. His leg is held together with a scaffold of extruding pins that catch on table legs and sheets and make him white, silent with pain. He complains never. He bites down, closes his eyes, and disappears from us all. He tends to his leg like a priest to a supplicant. He ministers to his pain with marijuana, takes himself off morphine four days after the accident. He tells the doctor, "I am an addict. I will die of the morphine long before I die from this leg."

Beware the mind.

He grows jasmine, gardenias on the balcony, coaxing little blooms from their plastic tubs. He grows himself a tiny fragrant jungle on a narrow shelf high above the city. He wheels himself from room to room, shuddering on crutches to meetings and doctor visits. He rolls tiny joints of weed that he pulls from a faded black nylon fanny pack slung at his hips so his hands are free for crutches. He smokes them like a pauper. His eyes grow small, red, beady. He is lucid, coherent, and forgets everything. His skin grows sallow, like a yellowing tooth, as the infection spreads through his blood. He finds a job, improbably, working for an international corporation looking to secure tenders for gas pipelines from the Argentine government. He is the liaison, a middleman again. He waits for deals to close, anxiously, nursing them like his miniature garden.

His wife retreats to her bedroom and her telephone and her television. She curls on her side and weeps at her shattered life. She is newly married, newly mothered. The baby toddles, then marches between them, the one bridge they can agree to meet on. Pain is utterly solipsistic. There is nothing but pain. There is no room for anything else, no room for empathy, for another's plight, for your wife crying in the next room, for your husband bent over his ruined body. His wife grows hard, depleted of compassion, bereft of love and lovingness. The baby grows loving, a peacemaker, an ally to all. My father grows self-sufficient, imperious, autonomous in his pain and self-medication. What his obsession has cost them all is too immense for him to admit, far less to apologize for. He is already paying a price so great he dare not complain about it. But he will not add to his burden by asking his wife's forgiveness. He will endure his pain publicly, but not his shame. I visit often. I sleep on the exhausted white sofa in the living room. I bring books for him, perfume for her. The air is heavy between them. They brighten on my arrival. Another bridge on which to meet. They laugh, drink the whiskey I bring them from the airport, share meals because I am there to join them. My father has a family again and I am part of it. I am loved and I am needed.

But I cannot stay. And my father cannot leave. He cannot leave me now. Cannot disappear for weeks and months on unaccountable trips. The lion is caged.

He turns to books to replace his lost life. At first I send anything that will engross. I send him thrillers, Grisham, Clancy, Harris. He reads them all. Too dark, he tells me. I send him Hemingway, spare and lean. He reads it. Too butch, he tells me. I send him Jane Austen. Delightful, he says, but what has it to do with me. I send him the travel writing of V. S. Naipaul and Paul Theroux. Ah, he says, at last. He reads and rereads these men, tracing their friendship and their falling-out. He travels with them, deep into the subcontinent, into Siberia, into Japan.

It takes him two hours to get his leg ready for bed.

My little sister clambers over me. She watches me with my

father but she does not care that I come. I am no threat to this little body. Her father never goes anywhere. She has never known him to be anywhere other than in his study. She only knows herself in his lap, or squirreled beside her mother in the other room. She has never known them to share a bed, or a bedroom. She has only known these four walls and that her father does not leave them.

After seven years of battle my father's infection rages so deeply that the doctors have no choice but to amputate. The rot has polluted his blood, threatens to kill him. They agree to preserve that delicate structure, the knee, and amputate below it. But when he wakes up the whole leg is gone. He has been left with six inches of thigh.

Pain

I EAT DINNER EARLY with the children. It is quiet, peaceful. My son, who is six, asks me with his wide eyes if my father would still be alive if he hadn't died.

"Yes," I reply. I know exactly what he means.

"How did he die?" he asks.

I look at him. He knows how my father dies. It is a story they both know by heart. I feel flustered, irritated.

"You know how he died, darling."

"He fell out of a window, didn't he?" he insists.

"Yes."

"Did he mean to?"

My daughter, my sea anemone, places her hand on mine.

"You okay, Mama?"

I stand up.

"I'm going to have a bath."

I walk to the stairs, come back, kiss my son on his head, and turn away before he can talk to me again.

I sit in the tub and stare out the dark window.

Later I tell my husband that I am struck by how hard it still is for me to talk about my father's death. I feel protective of him, of the violence of how he died, of the absurdity of it. It's a bad punch line to a terrible joke. There lingers, unspoken in the air, the possibility that he did it with intention. I cannot even type the words "on purpose." I cannot hold them in my mind. The idea that this is how his story ends, with this dull thud, feels too desolate, too dumb, too absurd.

My father can tolerate all pain as long as it is his. Mine is intolerable to him. He rarely deals with it. Ours is the love affair of the glamorous. We meet in Barbados, Lima, Cuzco, Paris, Buenos Aires. We have no chance to become routine to each other because repetition requires time, and we have none. Not for him the grind of watching me solve fractions, of filling endless summers, of inventing another meal. My father teaches me how to play backgammon, take a curve at speed, and make a Bloody Mary.

I am six. We are in Marbella, staying at a white hotel close to the beach. My father has rented a villa on the golf course and there is a nanny to look after me and my adopted sister. We have never had a nanny before. I don't remember her name. She has come with us. She has fiery red hair that she occasionally lets me braid if I am good. She wears the same thin black swimsuit for two weeks. It is low in the front and makes her breasts plump out the sides and high at the back which makes her buttocks plump out at the sides and all of us watch her and know we are meant to and not meant to, as she walks out of the pool, and flops on the hot stone, glistening and sleek. My father wears dark glasses but I can see him looking. At night the swimsuit drips like a sealskin on the veranda. At night there are fights in the room my father and stepmother sleep in. My adopted sister and I stuff pillows over our heads so we will not hear my stepmother's pain, my father's low tones. I wake to hear the front door slam and the crunch of tires on gravel. I wonder if he will come back or if I will be stuck forever in a white villa with two women who hate each other. We spend our days with the nanny. My father joins us for meals, sometimes. The nanny fluffs her hair in the mornings, picks at her melon, disappears in the afternoons.

At the hotel, across the golf course, there is a large shallow pool for kids. We go there in the afternoon. I play with my adopted sister. I am grateful for her company and frustrated by her age, her language, her newness. She is a puppy we haven't trained, still prone to nip. She is exciting, exhausting, frustrating. We lie on sun loungers bickering. I do not want to be in charge of her. I want a friend whose welfare is in her own hands. The shadows are long. The nanny has red eyes and a magazine. I see a girl with braids and a pink swimsuit. I can be her friend. I run into the pool, wading too fast down the wide steps of the shallow end, steps that are slick with a summer of sunscreen, and as I run, I slide, I slip, I fall and cut my head on the sharp edge of the step. The girl in the pink swimsuit screams. The pool billows with blood. I reach back and feel the broken seam of my head. The nanny is in the pool, wrapping me in a reddening towel, pulling me out, and my adopted sister is watching, mouth open, her arms straight down at her sides like a tin soldier.

I don't remember my father appearing, nor the doctor we visit. I don't know if he comes to us or we go to him. I am sitting in my father's lap and I call my mother to say good night, as I do every night I am not with her. I am in my nightie, the one with tiny roses on it, and I have a bandage wrapped around my head and I tell her I had a good day, a normal day at the pool. My father keeps a hand on my back, nodding, encouraging. I wish my mother would ask me, quite out of the blue, if I happened to fall and cut my head open that day, so that I can exhale, and cry and say, Yes, yes, that happened, and not break my promise. Because I have given my word not to tell my mother. He has told me not to. He has told me not to worry her. I am home in a few days anyway. She'll know then.

If we don't talk about it, it didn't happen. If we don't talk about it, we don't have to feel it.

The nanny disappears that night. Her room is empty the next morning. There is only a damp patch on the veranda where her swimsuit has dripped. My adopted sister cries, missing her. She tries to help me pack my suitcase. I am still dizzy. I cannot do it. No one ever speaks of the nanny again. I return to London where my mother takes me in her arms and says she knew, she knew something was wrong. The English doctor comments on the tightness of the stitching.

"Spanish embroidery," he says and sniffs.

I visit my father soon after his amputation. He is already home. He is lying in bed watching television, arms stretched above his head, propped up. He is not yellow anymore. His blood is clean for the first time in years. He beams, he reaches for me. I walk around the bed, eyes firmly on his eyes, unable to look at the vacancy below. I lie beside him. He tells me this is better, life is better, everything will be better now. He throws back the sheet, as if testing me, as if testing himself, to see who will flinch first. I do not flinch. He shows me the tiny thigh. The neatness of the stitching. As we speak it rises of its own accord, phallic, obscene, inexplicable. I am horrified. A reflex, he explains calmly. The body learning where it ends now. He pushes it down, covers it with the sheet.

My father's third daughter by his third wife is now a boy. To distinguish him from my brother, my mother and stepfather's child, I will call him my father's son. Today my father's son sends me a copy of some emails he has found in a drawer, an exchange my father loved enough to print out and keep. The email is from one of my father's skydiver friends, a man my father loved. The friend writes on hearing about my father's amputation. He writes about my father's courage, how he knows he'll see him soon, swinging a prosthetic leg around, doubtless skydiving again. In the email back to his friend my father talks about the "poker face" he keeps up when the surgeons break the news to him about the scale of the amputation. It is a poker face he keeps up for almost the rest of his life.

He waits months for the stump (that word, so thick and heavy on the tongue, deformed, abbreviated) to heal and then begins his long struggle to walk with a prosthetic. It is painful to read his friend cheerleading him, reassuring him with visions of marathons, parachute jumps, a fresh start, knowing the years of blisters, swollen flesh, heat rash are to come. His body is in shock. His body does not believe there is no leg there. Phantom pain ghosts his imaginary knee and his disappeared ankle. He is plagued by cramps he cannot touch. He lives with a poltergeist. The prosthetic leg lies largely unused, propped against a wall unless he must attend a formal event. He wears shorts, he sees fewer and fewer friends. He smokes more weed, keeps a banana (potassium, good for cramps) by the bed for when he wakes arching with a pain he cannot reach. He reads online that he must teach his brain to know where his body ends now. He props a hand mirror against his stump and stares at it while he drums the amputated thigh with his hands, insistent, drumming the new boundary into his muscles.

The amputation is meant to cut out seven years of pain and festered marriage. It is meant to be a fresh start. But instead it is a vacancy haunted by the past. The lopsidedness of my father's walk mirrors the lopsidedness of a family where my father takes care of his leg, and his wife takes care of everything and everyone else. Phantom pain, the memory of trauma, afflicts them all. I read and reread the letter from the fellow skydiver, seeing my father through his eyes. The vastness of the man, the idolatry of him, how beloved he was. He must have fallen like Icarus for these men.

My father teaches himself to drive a stick shift with one leg. He uses his crutch and a swift left foot in order to start the engine and put the car in gear. He is enormously proud of this resourcefulness. There is no money for a new car. There is barely money for a new leg. My father asks for his amputated leg to be cremated, and he keeps the ashes in a bag under the driver's seat of his car. My father's son tells me that if he stretched his feet in the backseat he could touch the bag with his toes. My father wants to scatter them at the airfield, but that never happens. Nobody is sure where the ashes of the leg end up.

I am forty-one. My father comes to visit me in Los Angeles. I want him to meet my son, who is nine months old. I pay for his flight, upgrade him with air miles to surprise him. I pick him up from the airport. He is on edge, dark circles under his eyes, his hair closely cropped, his face grizzled. I have never in my life seen my father unshaven. He leans over and kisses me.

"What's this?" I ask, caressing his face.

He strokes his stubble. He tells me his daughter likes it.

"She says it looks better. You don't like it?"

I hesitate.

"I'll get used to it."

"Well, I don't like your hair."

I feel slapped. My father has never criticized me. He has been in my car for less than a minute. I am at a loss. I scramble.

"How was the flight? Were you comfortable?" I ask.

He looks out the window.

"It was okay."

I wait.

He looks at his hands.

"They've changed everything. I didn't know how the seat worked. I didn't want to look like some idiot who'd never traveled before. I waited to watch my neighbor and see what he pressed to recline the seat or watch a movie. But he just put on his eye mask and went to sleep."

"You didn't ask for help?"

He looks out the window again.

"I felt like a clown. I couldn't make any of it work."

I reach over and put my hand on his. He takes it but keeps looking out the window.

The palm trees blur and twist into the gray corridor of the

freeway. It stretches out interminable with angry unmoving cars. I wish I were at home with my children. I wish he hadn't come.

We spend the week peacefully at home. We take the children to a playground where he pushes my daughter on a swing, higher and higher, her neck thrown back, her plump legs swinging, his hand steadying her as she flies. He hides behind a pole, pretending to be invisible, my daughter screeching at the joke, begging for more while I hold the baby, fatly smiling in the sun. We share water, ice-cold, and sliced apples and watch the hawks soar high above the hills and the children are happy, we are happy. Here he is, my invisible father. Here he is for my children to know. I am glad he came.

My daughter is in the hot tub. She asks my father to join her. He pinks with pride. He is wearing shorts with his prosthetic leg encased in a flesh-colored nylon stocking, a secretary's leg, with a tidy calf and a trim ankle. He goes to change, emerges in his swim trunks and walks over to the hot tub. He stops for a moment, reaches down and unhooks his leg, props it against the tub. I had not thought it would be so sudden. I have not prepared us for this. My daughter stares at him, stunned. She shakes her head, her mouth open. She wades to the side and hauls her little body out of the hot tub, unable to stay, unable to speak. I hold my arms out to her, to explain, to contain, to keep her with him. She skirts him as though he were a snake in the grass. She shakes her head, whispering to herself, unable to look at him. I have told her about her grandfather's leg but she is two, she has no words for what she has just seen. She is repelled, she is horrified. I soothe her, apologizing over her head to my father. I feel the heat of his embarrassment, watch him twist it into something he can manage, which is blame.

"You didn't tell her?"

"I did tell her."

He climbs into the hot tub and stares out at the ocean.

Every evening my husband makes him a cocktail the same color as the sunset and carries it outside to him. My father sits, his back to the house, looking at the vastness of the blue beyond and the fat stripes of orange and navy that bind it as the sun dissolves. I look up from the sink in the kitchen, where my baby sits for his bath, while at the table my daughter spoons peas on her head. From the sink with my children, washing bodies and plates so I can prepare my father's meal, I watch his shoulders sink, his breath slow, his chest widen. He needs this, I think. He feels at peace here. I have given him peace. He has never given me peace, I think. He does not deserve me, I think. I snarl the thought back inside me. Instead I yell at my husband, I throw a lamp at him, overwhelmed by laundry, by meals, by meeting the needs of a man who never met mine. Outside my father sips his drink.

At dinner he tells us stories. I have heard them all before. I don't remember them now. I remember only the light behind him, the way he folds his napkin and pushes his plate across the table for me to clear, the exquisiteness of his table manners, and the cracked mirror of his narcissism. I long for bed. I wonder why I invited him. I wonder how many years of my life I have spent longing for my father and now he is here and I wish he was gone. My husband, who lives for stories, leans in to his father-in-law. They adore each other. My father is grateful I chose a man who is loving, who is steady, who does not leave. He thanks him, often. I feel irritated, as though my husband has done us all a favor by marrying me. I clear the table, desperate for sleep, for a single question about how I am.

I would give all I have for another hour at my table with my father.

On his last night, he confides to us that his daughter has recently told him that she is gay. And that she is not a she but a he trapped in the wrong body. And that this new boy has chosen a new name for himself. And that his wife is in distress she is incapable of hiding. He is struggling. He is doing all he knows how to do, which is to love his child. He sighs.

"I love her. Him. Whatever, whoever he is. Maybe it's a phase. Maybe it's forever. But I love her. Him."

I nod, place my hands on his shoulders, and kiss the top of his head. This is why he feels so heavy. I watch him lay some of this weight down at our table. I watch him curve with fear and straighten with relief as he shares himself with us. I am proud of him.

The last day comes like a salve. I wonder if we are both

relieved it is over. It was the longest I have spent with my father in years. He packs his bag neatly, efficiently. He tours the house one last time and then sits in his favorite chair in front of the view as though to steep his bones in it. He points to the shed at the end of the garden.

"I'd like to live there."

I cannot tell if he is joking. Or if he is testing me. I do not want him at the bottom of the garden. After all these years without him I do not know how to live with him. I know how to miss him. I do not know how to tolerate him. I want him another continent away where I can manage the neglect. I smile and hoist his bags into the car.

I put my arm around his neck and pull him toward me, to take a rare photograph of us together. I catch us both in the fading light, in the moment of farewell. His almond eyes glisten, are small. His cheekbones rise like small valleys against my face. He looks happy. He looks sad. He looks heavy. It is the last photo of us together.

We drive in quiet along the ocean highway. The white sand and low buildings and the sunset at our backs.

"This was the happiest week of my life," he says.

I wonder how this could possibly be true.

Two weeks later he calls to tell me that his wife is leaving him. She is done. She can take no more. She has been his nurse for sixteen years. It is time for her to reclaim her life. They need to separate, share their child and what little money there is. My father sounds bewildered, at a complete loss. Not the accident, not the operations, nor the amputation, had left him so unmoored. He can barely complete a sentence. I struggle to understand him. And then I realize. He is frightened.

I do not blame her for leaving. They live their lives in separate rooms. They are two boats adrift on the ocean. But I do not know what will become of my father now. I have just witnessed his domestic ineptitude, his utter reliance on others. He has no money to pay for help. I do not know who will take care of him now. My stomach shrinks at the prospect of having to figure it out. I promise him we will find a way. I resolve to send him some more books. Don't look up until you get there.

Months pass. We speak often. I send money. I call my mother, who tells me I do not have to, that he must manage his family, that I have my own to take care of now. I agree and send it anyway.

I am late for dinner with a friend. My father calls. I am distracted, searching for parking.

"I have something to tell you."

The sun is setting on Venice Beach. A shelter for homeless men blushes pink. A brown man leans in the doorway. His lips are moving. He is praying to his god.

"I have a plan. It will solve everything. I am going to commit suicide."

I pull over.

The brown man turns toward me, sun-scorched skin, hair on fire, lips aflame with spirit, eyes burning. His eyes scar mine. I can see my hand with its rings on the steering wheel. My other hand has reached up to the ceiling of the car as though I could punch my way out of it. A siren wails. A star falls.

"Are you there?"

I cannot breathe.

"It's the only way," he says.

He tells me he's talked it through with his doctor. He tells me he's researched it online. He tells me his debts will be forgiven if he does this, and this way there will be enough for his wife and child to live on. He tells me he is too old to go through divorce again. He tells me he's had a good life. He tells me there is nothing left for him now.

"Think of it like one of your husband's screenplays," he says.

I am a mine that has caved in. My mouth is full of rubble. I do not know how to address the obscenity of the proposition. I tell him he cannot, must not, he must not speak these words, he must not speak them to me of all people, he must not ever say these things again, how can he ask this of me, how can he ask me for permission to go, to disappear again, how can he tell me as though I were nothing to live for, how can he ask me to let him go, on top of everything else, I cannot be asked this. I push the ceiling of the car up with the flat of my palm as though to give my lungs the room they need. I hold up the sky with my hand because it is falling on my head. I am sobbing, I am beseeching, I am raging. The brown man in the doorway is nodding now, encouraging me from where he stands.

My father is quiet.

And then he soothes me. He shushes me like a baby. He rocks me to quietness, back to breath.

"It's okay," he says, over and over. "I won't go. I won't. Now I know how you feel."

I babble. I promise more money I will wire in the morning. I promise to call the next day and the one after, to send groceries, to send books, to visit when I can. I promise to help him find an apartment, a carer, anything, everything. My father purrs. He is fat now, with the reassurance of how indispensable he is. I am hollow. I have passed the test. I have held on to his feet as he prepared to fling himself out one more time. I have saved him. I am exhausted. We hang up. The man in the doorway has gone. I lean my head on the wheel.

Two months later he is dead.

Window

My FATHER IS IN BED staring hatefully at the French windows. He despises morning light. He needs utter darkness for sleep. His metal blind is stuck. He cannot pull it closed. It has been stuck for days. The room is flooded with harsh winter light. His flimsy airline sleep mask cannot contend with this. The long sheer white curtains hang like useless pant legs. The metal blind lives high in a recess above the window frame, lowers like armor. But it is wedged at an angle, will not budge. His wife has called the handyman, she says. But he does not trust her. She is leaving him, leaving this house, why would she call anyone. In any case, no handyman will come. This country. Nothing works. No one works. He rises from bed. He hops across the room. His leg is propped against his desk. No point putting that on. He is only going to take a look. He opens the French windows so he can stand directly beneath the metal blind, inspect what may be blocking it. The curtains soften, straighten in the soft wind. He leans against the safety bar that stretches across the windows at waist height to stop the unwary from stepping out. He cranes his neck to see. He will see better if he can be just a little higher. He hauls himself, one foot, two hands onto the safety bar. He lifts his hands above his head to reach the blind, to give it one last pull. He is proud. Look at him. Standing on a bar on one leg. No need for handymen. No need for ladders. No need for two legs. He will show his wife how little he needs. He will show the world. He pulls. He slips. He falls.

He is falling. It is winter, it is cool, the air.

Oh fuck, he thinks, I am falling what have I done I am falling, I am falling again again again what have I done again.

Funeral

EARLY. White light. White nightdress in the chilly kitchen.
Bare feet on wooden floor. Baby sprawls in the high chair.
Daughter yells for yogurt. Husband still asleep. Always asleep.
Coffee, teaspoon, resentment, yogurt. Phone rings. My father's
number. So early for him. A voice I don't know. He says his
name twice. My father's wife's brother. The brother of my
father's third wife. He is a policeman, I remember. I wonder
how he has my number. I am outside because the kitchen is
too noisy. On my doorstep. One hand on the lintel. White
brick beneath my fingers.

"*Su padre falleció esta mañana.*"

I do not know this verb. I only know *morir*. I think this
must be a policeman verb. I wonder what the root of it is. I wonder how I am in the garden now. He is still speaking. My feet
are wet. The grass is bowed with dew. Each drop is so heavy.
I am at the peach tree now. I am at the peach tree and inside
the children are crying and I am in a nightgown and my father
is dead.

I am in Argentina. I have no idea how I got here. My friend and her family meet me at the airport. Like a mythic creature with many arms they carry me to their home, set me gently in a bedroom long left by one of the six children. I sit on a sagging bed piled with soft dusty quilts. An old feather boa wilts on the back of the door. I cannot close it, cannot leave it open. I do not know where to be. My friend is beside me. I have known her since the cradle. I understand the depth of my loss because I see it in her wet face. Her small hand is in mine, useless and all-giving. I am leaden. I feel the familiar ache of not wanting to go to my father's house. I do not want to go there, to see, to know, to begin this new life where he is not. I do not want to be here without him. I do not know how to be in this city without him. I do not know what to do with the unbearable liberation of not having to see him.

But he is still here, he has not left yet.

I am in my father's house. His wife comes to me, holds me to her body. We hold each other up. She sways, I weep, we weep, we sway. She is already stronger than she was. Her hands tremble as she smokes. We drink red wine in tumblers. We do not go upstairs. My father's daughter who is now his son appears. I have not met him in this body before. He is beautiful, silent, full. He looks just like my father as a young man. He does not weep but holds me close then moves upstairs to be alone. His mother waits, turns to me.

"I will never not see it."

She means his broken shape on that rooftop.

I shake my head. I refuse to imagine it. I cannot free her from this image by sharing it with her.

We must write the death notice for the newspaper. She finds a pen, a pad. We clear space on the tiny dining table. I have never written a death notice in any language. I have no idea what it should say. She consults, copies, writes. I look over to the dark staircase. He was here a day ago. A day ago I would have called up those stairs to see if he needed anything. I would have climbed them balancing books, wine, and cheese for him. He would have met me at the top, one hand on the banister, the other outstretched to cup my cheek and draw my face to his to kiss it. But today the stairs are silent. Some days he only comes down once, prepares food, and then drags himself back up. He and his wife do not speak. Their son shuttles between them, ferrying his love up and down, up and down these flights.

Now I am in his room. It is at the top of the house. He calls it his bunker. It comprises a bedroom, a bathroom, a closet with a mini fridge to save him from the stairs, and a little terrace where he can do his yoga and one-legged headstands. His world is here, his desk, his television, his books. This man, who swept the globe, now lives with a bidet and dusty minibar for company.

The white curtains breathe and curl in the breeze.

I walk to the bed. His glasses sit atop a book on the bedside table. They are smeary, his fingerprints still on them. The book is a collection of short stories I gave him when he came to visit me in Los Angeles. Inside the cover, in pencil in his tight handwriting, he has written the date and my name. I skim the story he has been reading. It is about a father who visits his son in college and their inability to connect. It is about a parent and child who cannot close the gap between them. I close the book.

His prosthetic leg leans against his cluttered desk. An old desktop computer dominates the space. It is surrounded by little piles of paper, invoices, bills and more bills. Beneath the stacks of paper, imprisoned beneath the glass, are photos of all his daughters, the dark-eyed and the blue, and one of himself frozen midair in a red jumpsuit, legs frogged, clouds massed behind him, eyes wide, thumbs up, and beside it, one of him and his third wife, their arms slung around each other's shoulders. I open his drawers, carefully, tentatively, as though he might walk in at any moment. They are filled with knotted plastic bags, rubber bands in a small silver box, paper clips, crayon scrawls and drawings by his child, and yellowing instructions for cameras, faxes, phones. In a bottom drawer, a plastic bag full of magazines and clippings from my acting career. I tip them on the bed, sift through the pages of my young smiling face, a dog-eared magazine I had no idea he had kept that featured a photo of me and him together.

I walk past his small but immaculately ordered bookcase, arranged by author, and wander into his closet. No more the softly illuminated shirts, each in its own sliding drawer. This room is dark, and dust motes float in the single beam of light. Faded piles of shorts and carefully folded sweatshirts. A row of untouched suits, the shoulders lightly faded from the skylight overhead. A scant bottle of whiskey sits on a shelf next to a slice of brie stiffening on a plate. It is private in here, a place of hoarded pleasure carefully administered. I am trespassing. I think of my fridge, bulging with uneaten food, leftovers, takeout. I feel ashamed of my plenty beside this palpable lack. He has so little to sustain him. The very air feels thin. I come back into the bedroom.

The white curtains shift and murmur.

The window is still open. No one has closed it. The metal blind, still askew, glints like a guillotine. Beyond is the brilliant hard blue city sky. Rooftops. Vaulted, flat, tiled, and cement. Aerials, sagging electricity cables, and air-conditioning units. A few treetops burst through the skyline. I look down. Twenty feet below me is a flat black rooftop, split by a broken white pipe.

I take the book of short stories from beside his bedside and the round silver tin full of rubber bands.

The white curtains shudder and flare as I close the door behind me.

Someone, I forget who, tells me they searched for a note. In case it was not an accident. In case he chose this death. No note is found. I don't know if there is one to be found. I don't know if he chose this death or it chose him. He would not have chosen a death so violent, I think. He would not have run the risk of a life of more incapacity, more pain. The death he described to me was a slipping away in sleep. Not this. No one wanted this. But somewhere as he slipped and fell I pray he felt relief.

I sleep long and deeply in my borrowed bedroom. For the first time in years I have no children to wake me. I am sodden with tiredness. My friend wakes me with coffee. We are late for his funeral.

We tear through the city. My friend's parents bicker about which route to take. I sit in the back, watching the city, grateful for the love of these people, grateful to be taken anywhere, to not have to navigate anything more than how to sit upright. I do not know how to be anywhere. I am floating at a little distance from myself. We pull up at the cemetery. We have no flowers, nothing to offer but ourselves.

"Go," says my friend, "I'll buy some."

She disappears. I feel panicked without her. Her mother places her arm around me, shepherds me toward the church. I have never been here, never attended a funeral that was not my grandmother's, never set foot in a cemetery that was not a tourist attraction or a shortcut. The chapel is so cold. There are scarcely twenty people here, scattered among the pews. So few, I think. This is not enough. I feel embarrassed on his behalf. And then I feel ashamed that I am embarrassed of him even in death. My father's son is bundled in a thick coat. He is wearing my father's cap. My father's wife squeezes my arm. Six men bring in his coffin. My cousin is one of the pallbearers. I cannot look. He cannot be in that uncertain, wobbling case. He would refuse. I refuse. I turn away and the howl rips out of my chest. I bury myself in my friend's arms. She and her mother throw their bodies on me like blankets on a fire. My father's son is white, silent in his mother's embrace.

The casket slides into a wall of vaults. The cold of the parking lot bites my ankles. An old friend of my father's hugs me. His coat is the softest thing I have ever touched. I rest my cheek on his shoulder. His wife watches me with gentle eyes.

"You were born of a great love," he says. "I never knew anyone as in love as your parents," he says in his beautiful black coat.

I wonder what we are supposed to do now. I wonder if I am supposed to have organized something, a wake, a party. People hover in the harsh light and get in cars, get back to their lives and their long weekends. I am numb with cold. It feels wrong to let them go. There should be food, drink, a closing in, a coming together. But I have nowhere to invite anyone. I roil in the familiar feeling that my family here never does things quite right.

My friend's mother, as always, steps into the breach. She sweeps her arms wide across my pale relatives and invites them all to her home. My father's wife and son prefer to go back to their house, to gather into each other's arms, in the silent rooms. I kiss them and we part. I am relieved to not have to follow them home.

It occurs to me that it is not my home now. Home, with my father, has meant so many buildings, so many countries. It is a word like an empty apartment waiting for him to take up residence. And now he is gone. I have made this pilgrimage to this city for my whole life because he is here. But now he is gone. I wonder if I will come again. I wonder why I would. To tour the ruins, show my children the outside of all the buildings that I called home.

Argentina is vast, disastrous, magnificent. My father disdained it. He was nostalgic for English order, civic duty, accountability, and while he longed for these things from his government, he knew that he and his people were incapable of them. He and his sisters would tut and shake their heads at the latest political scandal, roll their eyes at the inevitability of it all. I wonder if my father's disappointment in his country was his way of feeling his own failure to live up to his potential. Because my father is Argentina personified. A nation shimmering with promise brought to its knees with heartbreaking predictability by its own corruptibility and hubris.

We gather, my aunts and cousins, at my friend's family home, at the table, with hastily assembled food, wine, beer, conjured from corner shops. We drink quietly, then loudly. My friend's many siblings gather and offer me their love, their condolences. Stories fly. My aunt smiles and gasps through tears. She had spoken to him just hours before. My cousin, with whom I lived in my grandparents' flat all those years ago, shares adventure after adventure of my father's life. I marvel at all he knows. He spent more time with him than I did, this nephew, this surrogate son.

I walk the city alone the next day. I want to be alone. I want to experience myself alone in the city, with no children, no father, no husband. I want to feel as untethered as I actually am. I cry and smile and cry. I walk to my father's neighborhood. I do not want to go back inside the house. I meet my father's wife and her son for lunch at a restaurant. He steps away to find a waiter. She turns to me.

"He has not cried," she says. "He is hard like your father."

I hold her hand. I tell her that he will. We will all find our way, somehow. I tell them stories about my children. We fall silent. We have eaten many meals alone together over the years, waiting for him in hangars, in hospitals, downstairs hearing him thump around above. Now we are silent. I feel thinner than I have ever been. This winter can slice me like a pear. I pay the bill. I tell her what little there is to have of his belongs entirely to her and her son. I tell her, quietly, that I am done. She nods, understanding.

The next day my friend and her parents drive me to the airport. We are quiet. She wipes her eyes as she hugs me beneath a huge poster of a movie star in eyeliner and a cowboy hat.

"Come again soon. When you are ready. We are here."

The house takes a year to sell. For another year my father's wife and child live in that same house where he fell, with its broken pipe and silent third floor. It sells, finally, and they move into a small but pretty apartment in the center of town.

I have not gone back yet.

Lighthouse

I WRITE AND WALK and write and walk. I listen to audio-books as I walk along the cliffs that stretch beside the ocean. I find I want only Virginia Woolf to speak to me. I listen to *To the Lighthouse*. The waves of her prose wash over me. I feel her longing to express the truth of how much a single moment can hold. I hear her conjure the illusion, that miracle of simultaneity, of what it is to be alive, to serve soup, to be a mother, to hear the thrum of war, to feel the present become the past like the cling of a cobweb across your face as you move through a doorway. I tread the path along the shore and watch the traffic and imagine a little boat making its way to an imaginary lighthouse, full of a broken family.

This is what life is, I think. It is all things all at the same time.

I used to say that being loved by my father was like being loved by a lighthouse. It went dark for a very long time and then you were dazzled by the stroke of the glancing beam. But I have come to realize that I was the steady one, searching the dark water in order to find someone to save. He was the waterlogged craft, sometimes capsizing, sometimes afloat, that crept along the shoreline, hid in headlands, braved the depths, foundered on every rock. I think it is our job as children to move away from our parents. And it is theirs to remain steady, to remain constant, at least to us. My father was consistent only in his inconstancy. I was his lighthouse. And my mother was my rock.

I rarely dream of my father. He visits me as infrequently in death as he did in life. A month after he dies I dream that he has called me. I do not get to the phone in time and he leaves me a message. His disembodied voice crackles from an old-fashioned answering machine. He tells me that he was sorry he had to leave so soon and would I mind paying his American Express bill. I wake laughing out loud.

Last night I dream of him again. It has been years since I heard from him. I dream I am in his city for the first time since his death. Everything feels foreign, strange. I sit at his sister's, my aunt's, kitchen table, looking out at her lush garden in which, inexplicably, stand an oven and a sink. She prattles at my back, explaining the convenience of her jungle kitchen. I feel empty. I wonder how long till I can leave. I wonder why I have come back. And then, with the ineffable simplicity of dreams, my father is beside me, seated at her kitchen table. He is there, solid, a lion to my touch. He reaches his arm around me and gently pulls me onto his broad chest. My head lies against his laundered soft white shirt, one of the old ones, the good ones.

I feel him breathing, I feel the three tiny woven initials that lie over his heart pressing into my cheek. I inhale him. I weep as he holds me to him. And then I wake. And then I weep again.

It is a blood moon eclipse tonight. The children are in bed. I have read, ministered, tucked in, supplied, and declined. I have finished with them. I watch a television show in bed. It is a show I am in. Everyone is trying to get to the red planet. No one knows how to do it yet. The bedroom door opens. My husband enters. He is carrying binoculars.

"I'm showing the children the eclipse. I'll put them back to bed once it's over."

The door closes. I frown, I cluck, I wonder if I should go and look at it. No, I think, no, I want this for myself, not that. He wants that. He can corral them back to bed when he is done, I will not, I am done with that. Satisfied, I furl back in bed, to my screen. The door flings open again. My daughter is here, breathless, a coat swinging over her nightgown. I must come, I must see this. I sigh. Together in our white nightgowns we stride up the driveway, to where my husband has set up the telescope. My son hops from foot to foot. He is shivering with excitement. I look up at the soft dusky moon. It is milky orange like a setting sun, like the red planet. It looks down at us, in our driveway. The telescope points back at it like a gun. I bend down to it. There it is, a red planet, only this is the moon, our moon, bathed in a sunset. There it is, so familiar and so unknown. A lighthouse seen close and from afar. There it is at the top of my driveway, not in my screen, and here are my children dancing from foot to foot, now in my arms hot and burrowing. And here is my husband who sets up a telescope on a hilltop and does not care about bedtime but only showing them things. We carry them back to bed and they are lambent, arms full of love, grateful.

Perhaps I would have shown the children a photograph in the morning. Perhaps. I might have shown them a newspaper article about what I had let them sleep through. I would not have done this. I would not have thought to lift them from their beds, to toss that image before them. I know how to keep safe, how to tuck in, how to keep chaos at bay. I am still learning how to bathe in the soft hue of a blood moon.

SONYA WALGER began her career as a film and television actress in 1998. Known for her roles on television shows such as *Lost* and *For All Mankind*, she studied English literature at Christ Church, Oxford, and is the host of the literature podcast *Bookish*.